WHERE THE BIRDS HIDE AT NIGHT

WHERE THE BIRDS HIDE AT NIGHT

GARETH WILES

Matador
9 Priory Business Park
Kibworth Beauchamp
Leicestershire LE8 0RX, UK
Tel: (+44) 116 279 2299
Fax: (+44) 116 279 2277
Email: books@troubador.co.uk
Web: www.troubador.co.uk/matador

ISBN 978 1783063 659

British Library Cataloguing in Publication Data.
A catalogue record for this book is available from the British Library.

Typeset in 11pt Book Antiqua by Troubador Publishing Ltd, Leicester, UK

Matador is an imprint of Troubador Publishing Ltd

Printed and bound in the UK by TJ International, Padstow, Cornwall

A special thanks to my friends Claire and Ross

He was trying to escape his backside,
The way he walked.
He would gallop along,
That great weighty sack above his legs
Bouncing gallantly after him.

His head bobbed too,
When it wasn't turning to glare
Upon that meaty encumbrance usurping
His otherwise trim silhouette.
Pigeon boy flounced.

HOW NOOSE GOT THERE

Noose flopped back in his seat and thought: Sod off world, I can't be arsed with you today. There was good reason for thinking this. He'd had a lot on his plate lately – the remains found under Neville's bed being identified as Peter Smith and the murder of Inspector Kennedy, to name but two. He just wanted to put the whole thing behind him, and move on. It was all rather inconvenient, this whole affair, especially seeing as it involved the murder of a fellow inspector at the station. Kennedy had been chopped up into little bits and dumped in a plastic recycling bin outside the local Myrtleville supermarket. Peter, of course, had been dead for years. A colleague dead. A friend dead. A little upsetting, really.

He checked his watch, catching a brief reflection of his awful grey face in it. He hadn't been living these past few years. He'd been existing, in a word, drawing in enough oxygen through his vacant maw to sustain continued existence. It *was* a maw – he felt within himself a culmination of a lifetime's worth of failure after failure. He'd failed his colleague, he'd failed his friend and, above all else, he'd failed his family – failed them so many times. He felt he'd become just like Peter Smith, turning his back on everything that had proven too much of a challenge. Thoughts of his family now came to the fore in his mind – something he didn't want to think about right now. Perhaps he was angry. Yes, he *was* angry. All those years Peter was missing he'd been able to paint him as some sort of victim of fate in his mind. Now his body had turned up

– his final position on this planet confirmed – Noose brought back all the bad Peter had done. That he may well have been murdered by Neville, and a victim after all, was not what Noose was thinking about. He was thinking about how Peter had torn his family apart. The obsession with that man had cost Noose dearly. And, here he was obsessing again. No, he had to clear this whole thing from his mind. To think about his family, then – and not Peter – was perhaps a good idea.

A potential ending to Noose's day was going home, alone, right now or staying here in his office. He could trawl through all the documents on his desk, re-reading the same old files about the same old people. That Lucy Davies' killer was still at large troubled him again momentarily, but she was just one person in a long list of names that swirled around his head. Just names, labels, now. Another option to see Noose out for the evening was going out to a bar. This was alien to him – he had long given up socialising. The last real socialising he'd done was with Peter, and that hadn't exactly been the height of human interaction. That name again! Noose just couldn't shake it from the forefront of his mind. Perhaps the biggest trouble of this whole debacle was that Peter had clearly died never knowing who had murdered Lucy. He just knew Peter would have been in touch had he discovered the culprit. Unless, of course, the person had also done Peter in too. No, Noose just didn't feel that was what had happened. For some reason he sensed Peter had taken his own life. Did any of it matter now? For a detective inspector, Noose felt strangely disinterested in solving crimes at this very moment in time. All he wanted to do was get the weight of life off his back. It was all bogging him down a bit.

Slowly he got up from his desk and ambled towards the door, stretching his hand out to take a hold of the handle. He looked down at his hand, the fingers unable to flatten out without due effort. All his fingers on both hands curled in towards the palm when not in use. Age, perhaps? This worried Noose... this terrified him. He was getting older, and his life was shit. No, he wasn't really bothered anyway. Everybody's life was shit if you gave it some thought. Nobody had the perfect life. Even if they believed they had, something always came along to spoil it. Noose had been witness to, and experienced firsthand, all that. His job had allowed, or should that be forced, him to see all manner of horrors. Always he'd been left, when those who'd either been the victim or the criminal had buggered off, to his own devices. Memories, forever in his brain, accumulating. Each family Noose came across had only lost, say, one individual. But, he had to experience this over and over again, day in and day out. Endless people. Of course, it was their actual loss of a loved one and their suffering would continue for the rest of their lives. It was confined to them, though. For Noose, standing back and looking in, it had left him with an overwhelming anguish towards humanity. Hatred, if you will. Humans just didn't help themselves, and it was supposed to be his job to help them – help they mostly didn't want. He opened the door and stepped into the corridor. Superintendent Hastings was standing there, about to have walked in. His bright white hair caught the fluorescent tube of light on the ceiling and shone down, causing Noose to pull back. Lost in his own little thoughts, it was the only indicator to the man that his superior officer was trying to get his attention.

'Another bloody murder,' Hastings sighed, thrusting a sheet of paper in Noose's face. Noose was away with the fairies, moving his weight from one leg to the other as he pondered his existence in his office doorway. 'Henry you twit,' Hastings barked. 'A corpse, delivered to death by the hands of a fellow man,' he went on.

'Or woman,' Noose uttered.

'What?'

'Delivered to death by the hands of a fellow man… or woman,' Noose went on, scratching his head. 'That's exactly what Peter would have responded with.'

'I haven't got time for this, just get down there and get on the case.' He pulled the paper away as Noose started to look interested. 'You *are* up to this, are you not?' He turned and rubbed his chin. 'Considering all the shit that's been hitting the fan around here of late, I do wonder.'

'It's a very large fan, Sir, but I can cope,' Noose responded, snatching the paper from Hastings' hand. He quickly scoured it and suddenly gasped. Confounded, he read the dead body's address again.

'Something wrong, Henry?' asked the tired, and rather old for the job, superintendent.

'Nothing, just this address. You do recognise it, don't you? It's next door to-'

'I'm well aware of the location, coincidental or otherwise.' Hastings placed the fingers from both hands around his neck and moved his head from side to side as a pained look befell his reddening face. Despite his age, his face was not sagging or especially wrinkled. He'd clearly been lucky, or just led a healthy life. Whisky was something he enjoyed consuming regularly, though it appeared to have done him little harm. A stiff neck, then, appeared one of the few signs of advancing years. 'Just go and sort it out, will you. It'll get your mind off the Kennedy case.'

'Yes, thanks.' He started down the corridor. 'Who's on that?' he called back as an afterthought.

'Nicola Williams.'

Noose blinked heavily.

* * *

Pulling up outside the house, for a moment he stayed in his car.

Looking across as police officers cordoned off the area and Lauren made her way inside the building with her toolbox, Noose cleared his throat and spoke to himself: 'Come on, Henry.'

'Sergeant Helen Douglas,' a gentle voice called out. Noose turned and looked out of his side window to be met by two piercing green eyes staring intently at him. He got out and slammed the door shut, making his way to the house as Helen followed. 'I'll be working alongside you on this investigation, Sir,' she continued. Noose wasn't particularly happy – all his other sergeants had met awful ends. He kind of didn't want to get attached to this one from the outset, so the best thing was to be very cold towards her. Luckily, too, he had developed an inability to recognise beauty – it had gotten him into a lot of trouble in the past – and so hadn't registered his attraction to this young woman.

'Call me Noose.' An officer lifted the police tape and the pair walked up the path.

This semi-detached house did not loom large physically by any means, but to Noose it felt terribly encroaching. All he could do was keep up his pace, focus forward, and enter. Once inside, he thought, the house next door could not see him. He was right, for once safely in the hallway he lightened up tenfold and turned to Helen.

'This is my first murder case as a sergeant,' she said with a little trepidation. 'I've been trained to brace myself for a horrible sight before I enter the murder scene, but I've witnessed a lot of awful things.'

'Mutilated genitalia?' Noose questioned lightly, grinning. 'Decapitated bodies where the perpetrator has excreted down the exposed neck?' he continued, trying to shock her.

'Much worse,' she replied softly, her short and lightly tubby frame remaining so fixed as to somehow leave Noose feeling intimidated. He backed away from his new sergeant, bumping into Lauren, who rushed past clutching her mouth with a gloved hand. She collapsed at the door, vomiting all over the step. As Helen went and put her arm around the heaving pathologist, Noose stepped into the room she had just galloped out of. Initially he was stunned, unable to register the sorry sight. He turned away, crying in despair.

'Who could do that? Just a child,' he sobbed. Helen got up and came for a look.

'Must be some sick, sick pervert on the loose, Noose,' she sighed whimsically at the bloody chaos. Her glibness did not register with him, he was too lost in sorrow.

Lauren got up and turned to face him. They both almost looked through each other, like they were hoping to see something more than just each other – something less hollow. There was nothing else to be seen. Everything else was gone, it was just the two of them now. Never really that close, or that distant, it felt false to try and manufacture some sort of bond or connection between just them now. There was something between them though, something remaining in the rubble left in the wake of Peter and Sergeant Noble. No, Noose didn't fancy Lauren. Far from it – he wanted to father her, to somehow protect and guide her. Still, it wasn't his place and regardless of his desires she didn't seem to need fathering. If anything, she was stronger than him. Perhaps he wanted her to mother him? Mother, or smother – anything to put him out of his misery. Speaking of attraction, he now focused on Helen and allowed himself to take her face in for the first real time. He desperately needed a distraction from the disgusting murder scene he had seconds ago been subjected to. Helen was indeed rather appealing, he thought for just a second, not allowing himself to venture too far down such a road as developing emotions for the woman. Well, to him she wasn't even a woman – she was a girl. Half his age. He felt so old, and yet he wasn't. He felt he'd lived for an eternity. Too long.

Helen turned and the last of the autumn evening sunlight

pouring through the front door caught her chubby cheeks. They were quite hairy, in a way – fair, downy hair. The shade had hid any such nuances to her face, and Noose again allowed her physical form to occupy his mind. He wished to be given the opportunity to explore more of her hidden features, be they physical or even mental. After all, he still considered himself a purveyor of *whole* women. This was his attitude, anyway. It was still very much the object that he thought of. She smiled at him as her eyes flicked down to his mouth.

'I've never seen a worse sight,' Lauren uttered, composing herself in readiness for going back into the room. She rubbed at her eye. 'Eyelash,' she mumbled, rubbing harder and harder until it was bloodshot and extremely sore.

'Where are the parents? Who found the body?' Noose asked almost rhetorically, staring out of the door. A police officer came from upstairs, his face as white as a sheet. Lauren just flicked her eyes towards the stairs and Noose cleared his throat, turning to them.

Up he went, Helen following closely behind. Another officer was standing on the landing just outside one of the bedrooms. He nodded to Noose, uttering 'Sir,' before moving aside and ushering the inspector in. Inside lay the dead little girl's young mother – naked and violated, with her tights tied tightly around her neck. Noose stared down at the faded pink carpet, his vision blurring as he pressed furiously on his temples with his thumb and index finger. 'Danielle Henderson. Single mother. Father of the child is in prison for rape,' the officer informed him. 'Next door neighbour discovered the bodies.'

Noose got his mobile phone out and sent Hastings the text message: "2 corpses".

* * *

As Noose stepped out of the house a voice called to him from next door: 'Nearly twenty years my daughter has been dead. Twenty years and you got her killer acquitted.'

'Peter's dead too,' Noose called back, his shoulders sinking.

'So I've heard. Even in death he taunts my family still.'

Noose turned to face his aggressor. She, who could once have been a tall smart woman, stood stooped in her doorway with greasy dyed brown hair. Her white roots pierced from either side of the wonky parting atop her head and caught Noose off-guard. He felt somehow responsible for this mess in front of him and tried desperately to block her from his mind. She couldn't have been more than very late fifties by now, but looked a lot older. Noose did not exactly register her features, he was more concerned with bottling the sensation of dread and pity clutching at his brain.

'I understand you discovered the bodies?' Noose questioned her for confirmation.

'Yes,' Anna Davies replied, her eyes red and moist. 'Two more young lives taken away so horribly, just like my dear Lucy.' She tried to straighten her back, keeping her glare on Noose, hardened to the fact her daughter was long gone. 'Dani is like a surrogate daughter to me… was. Beth was the most wonderful granddaughter I could have wished for. Both gone.' She dropped herself onto the low wall separating the two gardens and sighed. 'I guess I just wasn't meant to have a family.'

'I was sorry to hear about Arwel,' Noose replied automatically. He, of course, had slit his own throat about a year after his daughter Lucy had been murdered.

'Yes,' Anna responded coldly, 'of course you are.'

Noose turned to move away as Helen watched with increasing delight at this uncomfortable exchange. 'A bereavement counsellor will be around this evening to help you,' he told Anna as he walked towards the gate. She just laughed.

'What was all that about?' Helen asked as they reached Noose's car.

'What was *what* all about?' he questioned calmly, turning to her and smiling falsely as he jangled his keys. Helen grinned back, silent. 'It's what happens when you're a policeman as long as me. There are cases that get complicated... cases that stick with you.' He turned and frowned, his shoulders sinking. Helen saw his face reflected in the car windscreen.

'I see.'

'Do you want a lift or something? Where are you headed?' he asked her, dropping any false smiles of happiness.

'I was thinking of popping into town for a quick drink.'

'After what we've just witnessed in there?' Noose replied, a little stunned, turning to look back at the house of horror behind them.

'I never mix work with pleasure.'

'Do you not?'

She came out with: 'Fancy joining me?' whilst sticking her hands in her pockets.

'I see,' was Noose's response as he scratched his chin. 'You not meeting up with some handsome young man then?'

'I think young men are rather stupid.' She stepped past Noose, opening his passenger door without a moment's contemplation. 'It's just a work drink, *Sir*. If we're going to be working together we need to get acquainted.' She got in and slammed the door shut, busying herself by belting up as Noose got in the other side.

* * *

'So what *is* all this business with that neighbour?' Helen pushed, leisurely bringing her half-empty wine glass to her lips. 'What did she say her dead daughter's name was – Lucy?' She sucked at the glass, extracting some of the liquid it contained. Noose topped it up for her, spilling a little on her hand.

'I'm ever so sorry,' he gulped as she put the glass down and he took her soft hand to wipe it clean with a napkin. 'You've never done a day's work in your life,' he gasped drunkenly, rubbing her smooth fingertips. They both laughed.

'My hands have done all kinds of jobs in their time,' she retorted, pulling it gently away from Noose's in order to pick her wine glass up again.

'Not many young women like red wine, I'm quite impressed,' he uttered, leaning in and staring longingly at her. His hands now rested boyishly on his lap as his head moved about loosely.

'How often do you take young women out for a drink?'

Noose laughed. 'Good question.' He looked up to the heavens, screwing his mouth up in feigned puzzlement as he pretended to recall. 'Not even my ex-wife was ever young!'' Noose suddenly blurted out, falling into a fit of hysterical laughter. 'Ten years older than me.' He sighed, lost in painful memories. 'Her father begged me to marry her, lest she be left on the shelf!' He picked his glass up and limply raised it to his lips. 'Trout could have kept her for all I cared.' Taking a large gulp of wine, his face relaxed as he sighed in relief.

'Did you ever take Lucy out for a drink?' Helen kept on, moving closer to him over the table. 'Is that why her mum is so angry at you?'

'Lucy was involved with a very close friend of mine – a troubled friend.' Noose filled his glass up to the top and drank half of it in one go. 'He's dead now.'

'I saw it all on the telly,' Helen responded. 'He wrote that book, then was going to commit suicide live on TV.' Noose did not reply. He wanted this particular discussion to end immediately. Helen sensed this, edging away and briefly looking around the bar at the other drunken strangers before deciding on another tact. 'If we're going to be working together, we need to get to know each other.'

'Why?'

'It will bring a healthy dynamic to our working relationship,' she explained.

'No it won't, it'll just complicate things and I'll get attached.'

'Do you not like getting attached? Are you afraid of being hurt?!' She laughed at him, grabbing his hand and squeezing it tightly. Initially he struggled to get away from her grasp, frustrated at her head-on attack. But, someway between her starting this and the eventual outcome, she came into the light above their table and he again caught a clearer sight of her arresting beauty. It was raw, unfettered in its acceptance of what it really was. Suddenly he regarded her very highly indeed, drawn to her sheer determination to just be who she was. At least, that's how he saw it. He let his hand take hers. 'You'll never have to get attached with me. There are no strings attached,' she said.

'I have a lovely Côtes du Rhône back at mine,' he suggested, raising the glass back to his lips. He kept on at it until well after it was empty, too far gone to even care. Rather, he found it quite funny and let out a little grin. Helen just pressed her finger to the side of his mouth and giggled.

They both rolled out of the taxi, full of burps and giggles, and just managed to get inside the house before collapsing in unison on the sofa. Helen, although she'd never stepped foot in here before, seemed rather at home. She cosied up to her superior with ease, he accepting and allowing her to do so. They felt the warmth of each other, needing it after the chill of the night air, and stayed close on the sofa for a while without speaking. Suddenly her arm flopped onto his leg and he jumped up. 'Wine!' he gasped, hobbling off towards the kitchen. She got up and followed, turning the light on for him as he fumbled around in the dark. 'Corkscrew,' he mumbled to himself as he searched in the cutlery drawer.

'How long has it been?' she playfully asked him, thrusting her chest towards him as she leant back against the counter.

'How long?' he queried back, lost in his drunken quest to find the corkscrew.

'Since you've had a good screw?' she blurted out, straightening her back and stumbling towards him. He turned to face her just in time, pushed backwards by her weight. 'Let's fuck,' she giggled, slipping her jacket off.

'I'm your, your,' Noose thought, puzzling over an excuse. He couldn't think of one. She undid his belt and dropped his trousers to the floor. There, underneath, his penis momentarily ached for solace as nerves briefly pulsed through his being. It was indeed fleeting, blood rushing to harden it as Helen dropped to her knees and slipped it out of his underpants. 'What are you doing?' Noose questioned stiffly, a little taken aback at his luck.

'What does it look like I'm doing, dickwad?' she laughed, grabbing hold of his penis and placing it in her mouth. She masturbated and sucked, taking a break only from the penis itself to suck on his balls. His heart pounded, but not quite from pleasure. Overcome with trepidation, though still very much erect, he pulled away from her.

'No. I don't want to take advantage of you.'

'Don't be a retard,' she growled, getting up and slapping him hard across the face. Stunned, he stumbled back onto the kitchen table – his penis flapping about like a stray buddleia branch. 'I'm a big girl. Do you wanna pound the fuck outta my pussy tonight or not?'

He gulped and nodded, deciding it best to be honest with both himself and this strange open woman in his house. Slipping his shoes off and his feet out of his trousers, he led her upstairs and they systematically removed their own clothes before flopping on the bed. Rather lacking energy through vast alcohol consumption, they lay still for a time beside each other.

'You're very attractive,' Noose decided to say, thinking it the right thing to do.

This seemed to spur her into action and she knelt over him. 'Don't patronise me,' she fired, punching him in the face.

'What the hell are you doing, you crazy cow?' he howled, holding his bloodied nose. She merely grabbed his penis and started wanking it, dragging her nails hard down his chest with the other hand.

'Why don't you do it back, you stupid twat?' She pushed her face right up to his, spitting in his mouth. 'Show me what a tough guy you are, *Inspector*.'

He just couldn't hit her back – he wasn't that sort. But, he found himself swallowing her spit and wanting her to carry on this mad episode. Again she put his penis in her mouth – all of it this time until she was close to gagging – and dragged her teeth along it as she pulled her head off it. Noose writhed in part pain and part pleasure, perplexed at the unfolding session. Desperately he just wanted to penetrate her, missionary style. Soon he got his wish, as she pushed him aside and got down on the bed, opening her legs and rubbing her clit as she waited for him to keep up. 'I haven't got a condom,' he whispered.

'You'll just have to suck your wet tadpoles outta there once you're done then, won't you?' was her luminous response.

He pushed himself into her as she smiled, her eyes closing and her hands clenching his buttocks. Soon he felt something sharp running along the crack of his bum before her finger disappeared up his anus. He did not want to stop penetrating her so let her carry on. With every thrust he gave her, she now replicated with her finger inside him. Initially it was something awful and icky to him, but he found himself lost in the moment and as he climaxed he was overcome with the deepest burning joy he'd ever experienced in his entire life. They just kept on going until he was well and truly flaccid and it would no longer go in.

She got up off the bed as he collapsed onto it in exhaustion. She left the room and went to the bathroom, closing the door and putting one foot on the toilet. Looking dreadfully through herself in the mirror, she clenched her fist and began punching her vagina. Harder and harder she got, biting her lip as she resisted screaming.

* * *

It wasn't the daylight that wakened Noose. No, it was a banging headache – throbbing, rather. Worse than a mere hangover, it was almost like he'd been put into a heavy sleep by something he had been unaware he'd taken. As his eyes realised their surroundings, they caught sight of Helen's head down the bed. In fact, his flaccid penis was in her mouth. The problem was that it was just her head, and head alone, that was down the bed. Noose lay dead still for a moment, frozen in vast unfathomable grief and anger at the sight of this young woman's decapitated head fitted loosely between his naked legs. His hands were mucky with dry blood and she had clearly been dead a few hours – he could tell by the greeny colour and sag of her skin… and the smell. Green had always been a favourite colour of his. The green of nature's unspoilt landscape, even the gorgeous dark green of his mother's lawn all those years ago. No moss, no weeds – just perfect green grass.

* * *

As is always the case in situations like this, Noose found himself under suspicion of murder. After all, he had bruises on his face and claw marks on his chest – not to mention teeth marks on his penis. To all intents and purposes, an unbiased onlooker would have concluded that quite a struggle had occurred between the pair, considering the horrendous bruising between Helen's legs. As he now sat waiting in the interview room at Myrtleville police station, he kept looking down at his hands expecting them to still be clutching her head. He could still feel the weight of it in his hands as he moved it. He had had to move it of course, in order to get up off the bed and call the police. He hadn't called them straight away though, had he? No, he gave it quite some thought as panic set in when he came across the rest of her body in the bathroom. There was an absolute hell of a mess in there, with blood and gore flung carelessly about, and some of it had gone down the sink when he'd washed his hands. The bathroom was, Noose reasoned in between the chaotic maelstrom, where the murderer had done the deed. Yet, there was no sign of breaking and entering. Had Helen let them in? Noose contemplated trying to make it look like somebody had forced their way in, but luckily reality kicked in and he thought better of it. Maybe he had actually done it during some sort of sleeping attack on the girl? That's the fear that now occupied him.

He'd never really sat this side of the table for any length of time before, and he saw the room in a completely new light. What most seized his attention was the face on the carpet by the door that kept looking at him. The floor was covered in grey carpet tiles and he suddenly felt like tearing this specific one by the door with the face on it up. It was a man's face, one he did not recognise, but it just kept staring up at him with unrelenting malice. No amount of adjustment of Noose's look would change this mark on the carpet from a face. Who's face was it? Was it the killer who'd slain Helen under his very nose last night? Mother and daughter Dani and Beth Henderson also remained very dead, and Noose couldn't get his head around any of it. He'd given their terrible rape and murders so little thought. All he'd been up to was shagging this new sergeant of his, who'd ended up dead herself. He felt like a creepy old man who'd violated some innocent young thing. A thing, yes; just an object that had come bouncing into his closed little world and back out again as quick as that. Her life had come to a painful, undignified end and he'd slept through it all. If he *had* slept. Maybe he did do it.

Some serious thought needed to be put into all this. If he had done it, Noose reasoned, then he'd have had to have suffered some sort of illness that made people do bad things during their sleep. He'd certainly heard of cases where husbands, or wives for that matter, had accidentally strangled their loved ones whilst both parties slept. But, to behead someone? The murder weapon was one of his own kitchen knives, so it was not beyond feasibility that nobody else was involved. No signs of forced entry, no introduction of a foreign weapon – Noose could have done this. It didn't take him long to practically accept that he was the murderer and he began formulating ways of punishing himself. No, suicide was not an option – that would mean he would go unpunished in the eyes of Helen's family and the law. Quite soundly he laid out a plan of action for pleading his guilt and making the whole trial as easy as possible for her grieving loved ones. After all, that was the right thing to do. Then, he would live out his final years in prison, coming to terms with the violent act he'd been capable of whilst doing something so seemingly innocent as sleeping after a particularly stormy session of one-night stand sex. Maybe he would one day emerge from his long prison sentence and be reintegrated into society. Could that ever be possible now that he had this condition where he murdered people in his sleep? Obviously his life was over, if this was the case. He'd have to be locked up alone in a cell every night for the rest of his life.

He'd wasted his life. Not just this latest problem – because that's what it was to him, a problem – but everything about his life in the past. Things had been gone at in the wrong way, and it had led to unpleasant incidents and unnecessary changes. Problems could always be solved, though. Couldn't they? Whilst he sat here waiting he felt he had time to have a proper think about all this stuff. Here he finally was, the centre of attention at last and with good reason to study his own problems. Forever he'd taken everyone else's tragedies and issues on board, absorbing them like a flimsy stained sponge that should have been chucked out long ago. They had dragged him down, emptying their sordid baggage onto his shoulders as he'd tried to aid and manage their lives for them with "the law" as his bible. Now the roles were reversed. Should he seize this opportunity and empty all of his shit onto the next person to come through that door? Again he looked over at that door. There was the man's face, still on the carpet, looking up at him. Ignorance was not bliss, because this face had not gone away. Paying the face attention would not make it retreat either. Only getting lost in his own thoughts, and bringing old things to his vision to look at once more, would help block this face from view. And it did, for a moment, as Noose remembered blabbing about his ex-wife to Helen. Oh how he'd slagged the poor bitch off to the stranger. Would he really not have been arsed had Trout actually formed a relationship with her? Perhaps that would have been for the best, giving her the security and love she had so claimed she needed. Her father would have been pleased that at least some man had come to save her after Noose had done the dirty. Any man! Luckily her father was dead by then, and Noose escaped at least one rollicking. She had been such a drab wife, though, if that is any excuse and clearly Nicola Williams had filled a vacancy. He'd never loved his wife, and he'd never loved Nicola. He'd never loved any woman. This hurt him the most. He'd been close to his mother, of course, and in this respect it could be said he'd loved her. But that is a different kind of love, and Noose had long separated that portion of his affections from the desire side. He both longed to love and be loved at the same time, but as the years had unfolded and a number, albeit a small number, of women had passed through his life he'd shrunk back more and more in acceptance that he would not experience that kind of love. Naturally, as he entered middle-age, he was not without just cause to think this. The evidence was there when you looked at his shitty marriage and affair with Nicola. Even last night's romp with Helen was a case in point. Had he in any way led her on? He was unsure, but felt he had somehow taken sexual advantage of her – after all, how could a young attractive woman find him appealing? He was balding, tubby now and generally a bit grubby all round. There was no love involved in this bizarre one-night stand. It had all been about pleasure, and about pain. The whole thing had hurt Noose, certainly, and Helen hadn't come off lightly, had she? The pleasure had not been worth it, and the pain was all too unwanted to wish to dwell upon. Yet, he couldn't help but dwell upon it as he sat here waiting for something – anything – to happen. This whole thing had helped manufacture a rock and a hard place situation that he'd rather not have had to face.

That face on the carpet now looked even more defined. There were eyebrows, one raised, and a distinct curve to the lips. Noose could almost hear the face talking, with a sly lilt, about how funny the whole thing was. Noose didn't find it funny at all, and this face was mocking him. He got up and put his foot over the face, rubbing and stamping at it in the surety it would go away. Surely this face would go? It did not. Surety turned to hope, turned to rage, turned to despair. Acceptance was not forthcoming, but a blind resign delivered Noose back to his chair. He dropped in it, wondering how long he'd now been waiting here. He didn't care, so long as he didn't have to wait much longer. That thought suddenly sparked in him a desire to be kept waiting for infinity, never to have to deal with the predicament he was in. Was he even in a predicament? If indeed he hadn't beheaded Helen, which was still a possibility, he was a free man and could hopefully go about solving her murder. Perhaps they were linked to the Henderson slayings, and he could pool the whole thing together. This could be his chance to redeem himself in both the eyes of the press and in his own mind. Solve these crimes and be a hero! For so long he had thought himself a failure. Well, when all you read about yourself in the papers day after day is your shortcomings, is it any wonder? He needed to give himself a good shake, straighten his back and sort this pile of crap out. As if he had beheaded Helen in his sleep! It sounded such rubbish – silly, silly rubbish. Bad things had happened, but who cared? At least things *had* happened and his life wasn't just a long list of nothing. It all added to the bag, reminding him every so often that he was still alive. His lungs still drew in oxygen, and blood still slid through his brain and heart. He could still use his brain, too, in solving these latest three murders. Three murders – three little, inconsequential murders. Damn! Noose slammed his fist on the table and grunted at himself in exasperation. No murder was inconsequential, when he really sat down and thought it through; but he'd fallen into the habit of thinking a life was just a life. A life was more than just a bag of deady slush to be toyed with and discarded. Noose knew this, and what he hated was the fact he kept having to remind himself of this. That was the price you had to pay when you were exposed to murder after murder for twenty years. And there weren't just three murders to solve, there were countless. One still at Noose in particular was Lucy Davies. Would he too die before her killer was brought to justice like Peter had done? What did bringing to justice even solve? All it meant was more tax payer money going on sustaining the cosseted life of a cunt who didn't deserve to exist. Noose was angry, he needed to calm down. It didn't do to show too much anger in this sort of situation. And, he didn't want his fellow officers patronisingly suggesting he "calm down". That would be the worst thing that could happen right now. The face on the carpet had seen his anger.

Maybe the point of keeping him waiting was to let him stew; mull over in his mind what he'd apparently done. Equally possible was the fact that everyone was really busy, tied up with all these latest problems. Problems needed to be solved, and Noose was the man to do it. Was he even a man at all? That blasted Helen had punched him around and fingered him up the arse. Well, he wasn't too concerned about that... just a little. A niggle kept twirling around, egged on by the face's wry grin, and centred on Noose's perception that having had a finger up his arse would make him the butt of jokes at the station. The information would soon seep out into the lower echelons of the station like everything else. It didn't take a lot to get the lower officers chuckling behind your back, murder or not. His affair with Nicola had left vast unerring scars on his reputation and identified an emotional weakness in his character. Such flaws took many successfully solved cases to patch up, and even then they were only patched. Another event, however small, could so easily tear it off again and reveal the old sordid silliness. Noose had had plenty of those. And, then there were the unsolved cases to his name. Peculiarly, perhaps saying more about the police as a whole than Noose himself, these weren't as much of a scar as the affairs and the other personal problems. Police were only people as well, and people are very faulty. No, he was treated with mild pity and comforted over the unsolved murders as other inspectors either took the cases on or they were confined to the vaults of failure. Should he bonk his boss or take an unexplainable liking to the young Peter Smith, however, and he would find his credibility in tatters. Odd, eh? Really, really odd. It didn't do to either have sex or befriend people. That was a lesson Noose kept learning over and over again. With so many of the best lessons in life, sadly, he would keep on forgetting it and letting himself get dragged in again. Dragging in was exactly what had happened last night.

The more he thought about it, the more he felt Helen had somehow put herself rather forward onto him. Was it all an elaborate and cruel set-up? But why would she willingly go along with having her own head removed from the rest of her body? That is quite a commitment to make; though Helen had certainly come across as a very committed kind of person. Committed to helping ruin Noose's life, by the look of it. The sunlight had come around the corner of the building and now tried its best to look in through the high, narrow frosted window. The face could get a nice tan as the angle was just right to catch it. So much did it sun the face, that whoever it was started to bask in the delight and shared the joy with a string of inaudible words. How frustrating that these words were going unheard by Noose! He doubted they were important anyway, ignoring them for a while. But, as the sun shone and they persisted, he got up off his chair again and dropped to his knees, pressing his ear against the carpet in a desperate bid to pick up any sound. Was it a message of hope from divine intervention? It might as well have been Noose's own inner conviction, for it was as unbearably impossible to decipher. So close did his ear get to the face, that he felt a little nip on it and jumped up. That the face could have bitten him was of mild concern; that he'd put himself in such a situation where that could have occurred troubled him immensely. He was now completely overwhelmed by existence.

He collapsed against the wall and he cried there, sobbing to his heart's content about things in general. He'd become so numb over the years that this felt especially self-indulgent to him, and rather enjoyable. He was crying both at recent events and for himself overall and it was such a great buzz. There, on the floor against the wall, he blossomed into what he'd always hoped he would become; though he couldn't quite place what that was. He knew it, however, because he now felt good about things and wanted to thank the dead Helen for allowing him to reach this emotional peak of release. But, then he was awash with the ever-constant circle of realisation that it was not Helen but her killer who had opened him up to this sensation. The briefest of flickers in Noose's mind told him to congratulate the murderer on a job well done – luckily this passed and he was loathe to warrant it credence again. That's when the sobbing thankfully ended, and he winked at the face in dominance. It did not wink back – it *could* not. The everlasting period between Noose being told to wait in here and somebody coming to question him now felt ever-tightening and he renewed his efforts to encourage its arrival. Standing up and about to check the door, he changed his mind and sat back down again. He neither wanted to find it locked nor unlocked. Had it been locked, this would amount to him having been found guilty in the eyes of his colleagues already – had it been unlocked, an officer would no doubt have been standing guard outside and he'd reach the same conclusion anyway. He could not win, obviously they thought he had done it. Hard he tried to conjure up an image of Hastings coming through the door to relieve his worry and set him on the case, to no avail. Hastings was neither forthcoming, nor likely to be the one. It was not his place to anymore. That place would be filled by somebody lesser known to Noose, no doubt, so as to avoid any emotional connection during questioning. Questioning – hah! He'd already answered all the questions he could to the officers who'd answered his call earlier today. There was nothing more he could actually give, aside from making something up to satisfy the interrogator. Should he do that? Perhaps it was easier that way, avoiding endless circles and circles of mental crap.

The door opened and rubbed the face off the carpet. In walked Nicola Williams. There she stood with her wide brown eyes oozing their leathery impenetrability at her old flame, as he looked up and caught sight of her. He hadn't seen her for a long time – perhaps too long, perhaps not long enough. All he knew was that she was going to delight in all this. She was exactly the same as she'd always been, and he could tell in an instant that she had not changed. Well, he certainly thought that. He wished she had not changed since last they met, and her lack of physical ageing only added to this as a credible belief. Her hair, possibly, had changed style and was now much shorter and bobbed, but Noose really didn't recognise this much. He wasn't interested in hair – he was interested in getting right back down to business. Whatever that meant.

'So she was the one who initiated the sex?' she asked with as much stress on ridicule as she could muster in her cadence.

'Is that too far-fetched a concept?'

'There was something between us, once,' she said coldly, 'but now there's nothing. I'm here in an official capacity to question you.'

* * *

After he'd finished at the urinal, he stepped up to the sink and turned the cold tap on. Never did he like washing his hands in hot water. Either it got too hot too quickly and burnt his hands, or it ran cold anyway; so there wasn't much point even bothering with the hot water tap. Anyway, he knew that the hot tap at this particular sink – the one on the left – hadn't worked in eight years. He didn't really like washing his hands at all – but he did wash them. Well, the tips of his fingers. He didn't really like looking at himself in the mirror either, especially now. But, on this occasion, he gave himself a nod of acknowledgement before preparing to move over to the hand drier. It was now, at this exact moment in his life, that he saw his face for the first time. Yes, he'd sort of had a look at himself before now, but never really seen himself. There he was in the mirror, never exact but existing, and for all the world he was at once satisfied. He *could* give a crap what he looked like, and he looked alright. A foray into personal physical acceptance was just what was needed at a time like this – anything to occupy his mind.

The officer stood watching him was there "for his own protection", not to stop him "doing a runner". Noose wasn't necessarily under suspicion now, just under a glorified house arrest at the station. He smiled at Officer Jacobs – one of those men who looked rather feminine, but who got all the girls – and smiled. Jacobs, relatively new here, smiled back. Noose led the way out and was met by Nicola Williams in the corridor. Standing next to her was a young woman who looked like a woman, dressed in a suit. It suited her.

'This is Sergeant Helen Douglas,' Williams announced, introducing the well-tanned, black-haired female by pointing at her face. 'Been away on holiday, plane was delayed.'

'But, but…' Noose stuttered, staring at his new sergeant.

'Yes, that woman who stuck her finger up your bum then got beheaded wasn't who she said she was,' Williams continued drolly, her eyes never leaving Noose's face as she basked in his torment. Jacobs and Douglas tittered. 'She impersonated Sergeant Douglas.'

'Then who was she?' Noose demanded.

'We don't know. No idea.'

Williams smiled as Noose pulled her to one side. 'Now look here-' he started.

'Take your hands off me, Inspector Noose,' she growled playfully, 'or I shall slap a restraining order down on you.'

'You can drop all this bullshit right now,' he carried on threateningly as Jacobs stepped between the pair.

'Language, Henry,' she cooed.

'Look, you were the one who told *me* to keep this professional, and here you are doing-'

'Doing what, Henry? What am I doing?'

'Do you still have feelings for me?' he outright asked her.

'Feelings?' she laughed. 'I never did have feelings for you, you just served a purpose back then.'

'Back when, the first time or the second time?' Noose's mind was full of all their trysts so many years ago, especially their last time – on her office desk in this very station. She had been a superintendent back then, rising quickly through the ranks because of her brilliant brain. Here she was, a decade later, slopping along as a mere detective inspector again.

'There never was a second time, Henry,' she spat, turning away from him and lowering her voice. 'You pushed yourself onto me, I had to keep you quiet because of what was going on with Norman.'

'Ah yes, so that is what this is all about, is it? Getting revenge on me because I cost you your high-powered superintendent position?' Noose laughed in anger, shaking his head. 'Norman Trout, hah. It was your own fault, you were the one helping him with those fake documents or whatever. You should have been sacked altogether.'

'I paid the price, Henry, as did Norman. I'm just trying to make a difference now.'

'Well you're making that, alright. You're ruining my life.' He pushed Jacobs aside, marching off down the corridor. Jacobs dashed after him but bumped face-first into him when he stopped dead and spun back around after Williams burst out laughing. 'It was you, wasn't it? You murdered that little whore in my house last night!' he yelled, pointing at her from down the corridor. The real Sergeant Helen Douglas, rather wishing she'd stayed on holiday a little longer, looked uneasily at the notice board and pretended not to be paying attention.

'Run along, Inspector, you're making a fool of yourself.'

In came Lauren behind Noose and, upon seeing him, stepped back uneasily. He turned to face her. 'Lauren,' he said to her, smiling. She did not smile back. 'What's the matter?'

'A word, please, Inspector Williams,' she called out down the corridor.

'What's happened, what is it?' Noose carried on. He'd known Lauren long enough to sense she was not at ease – not that she had been at ease for a long time.

'I think I should speak to Inspector Williams first,' was Lauren's brief explanation to the eager Noose.

Williams came up to the pair, followed closely by Jacobs. 'Go on, Lauren.'

'It's the DNA results for the Henderson murders.' She looked away from Noose, but would not turn from him.

'Yes, yes, what about them? Do we have a lead?' Williams encouraged.

'Of sorts.' She cleared her throat, unsettled. 'The sperm found in both mother and daughter matches the sperm I took from the body of the female found in Inspector Noose's house.'

'I see.'

'What?' Noose laughed, sure he'd heard her wrong. Jacobs came and stood right behind Noose, ready for anything. 'No, no,' Noose carried on, shaking his head, 'this is getting ridiculous now.'

Lauren now looked at Noose and asked him: 'Did you do it?'

'Do what?' he shouted. 'What the hell am I supposed to have done?'

'How did your sperm end up in the bodies of Dani and Beth Henderson?' Williams questioned him.

'God knows. I can't believe it, it's a lie. You're lying Lauren, you must be lying. You've got it wrong,' he cried out.

* * *

'That's how I ended up in here,' Noose finished, staring blankly up at the cell ceiling off the top bunk. Underneath him on the bottom bunk lay his cell mate Alex, the nervous young one-time husband of Katie Edwards, who'd also found himself, much to his own confusion, in prison.

'Must be tough ending up in here when you were a cop yourself,' Alex mused, sighing that there were others also going through what he was. Noose just listened, noticing the face from the carpet was now on the cell ceiling. It stared down at him, that wry grin having a good look. 'So who *did* kill Dani and Beth Henderson, if you didn't?' Alex asked.

'That face,' Noose responded.

'What face?'

'The face on the ceiling.'

'Did the face on the ceiling also kill Lucy Davies?'

'Probably.' Noose closed his eyes. There the face was, inside his eyelids and all the time looking at him.

When I'm transferring to you
Reborn with Life renewed -
Only Residual.

As I die I know not why
Death denied corporeally -
Only Residual.

HOW ALEX GOT THERE

Alex had just about enough time to absorb the image before it faded. This one would fade, yes, but there would doubtless be countless others. They never got the same one back, it was always a new one each time. That was the beauty of a limitless supply of nubile young women – there would always be another to take her place when this one was gone. That it was they who were having the direct sexual contact with his wife was a bit annoying for Alex, but the fact that he got to sit in and watch was adequate for now. Sitting in at a distance, of course. He would always sit in the green chair in the corner, pulling at his half-flaccid penis as the latest woman licked his wife's vagina, or indeed rubbed her own vagina against it. Katie would be raging with orgasm after orgasm as this went on – providing Alex was in darkness in the corner. She knew he was there, but could forget about him as she went full throttle on the bed in the other corner of the room... so long as she couldn't see him. The little bedside light was always shining on the two women involved, letting Alex have a look from the green chair. The couple had tried to have sex ever since their wedding night, but to no avail. Every time they tried it just hurt Katie too much. Her vagina closed up at the merest thought of Alex entering her, and it was simply no good. This was the best sex life they could hope for together – she with some random female stranger, and he wanking in the dark. Not the best of things, but adequate enough. There was a woman who loved Alex once, and he knew it. But, he threw it all away to marry somebody who wouldn't even shag him. Why? He couldn't answer that, he simply couldn't. The other woman *was* Katie's best friend Emma, maybe that had something to do with it? Alex was the kind of guy who liked to eat all the chocolates in his advent calendar in one go, and that was that.

One day Alex was sitting in the green chair with his penis out when Reaping Icon appeared in the room. Reaping Icon stood for a moment over the bed, having a look at the unfolding sexual activity between Katie and the latest woman the couple had enlisted.

'Hmm,' said Reaping Icon, his face expressionless. Alex's face, too, was expressionless. It was the same face.

'What do you want?' Alex called out to the one who looked like a man – who looked like him.

'For you to shut up,' Katie replied, deep in breath.

Reaping Icon came up close to Alex and closed his eyes. 'You can see all that you want to see, if you look,' he said, before going away. Alex got up off the green chair and left the room as Katie carried on.

'This is ridiculous,' Alex said to himself in the bathroom, keeping his eyes from the mirror. 'Why oh why am I in this whole fucking mess?' Now he looked in the mirror. 'Come on then, where are you?' he called out for Reaping Icon. 'Show me, you bastard, let me see what I want to see.'

'What do you want to see?' Reaping Icon asked him, appearing in the bathroom.

'I don't know. Do you?'

'Do you want to see Emma?'

'I can see her any time.'

'Am I not being honest with myself?' Reaping Icon looked behind Alex in the mirror. Alex would not turn to look – he could not see anyone there in the mirror. 'The Space, perhaps?'

'What?'

'Do you want to see The Space?'

'What good will that do?'

'The world of good.' Reaping Icon smiled warmly.

'What is The Space?'

'It is the summation of everything that ever was, is or will be. And, everything is nothing.'

'Everything is nothing? That doesn't make sense,' Alex laughed.

'I can grant you access to The Space, Alex,' Reaping Icon went on, his smile gone. 'You can do whatever you so wish. Nothing will be beyond your desire.'

'And nothing is everything, I suppose?' Alex asked glibly, though with a hint of nerves. He had, nonetheless, eased in Reaping Icon's company.

'Tread carefully, for there is nobody who can stop me doing as I wish.'

'Then why bother me, why am I significant?'

'Because you are me, and I am you.' After this, Reaping Icon went again, and Alex collapsed onto the toilet in a fit of hopelessness.

This Reaping Icon – this mirage of a man who flitted in and out of his vision whenever he so chose to – had not figured heavily in Alex's mind up until now. But, here in the bathroom whilst his wife had sex with someone else in the other room, he found himself at the end of his tether and finally willing to embrace his own desires for a change. He'd always been a bit weak in the mind, allowing himself to get carried along, and now he could see that. Reaping Icon could change all that, for sure! Or, was it just another case of weak-mindedness? At this moment in time he didn't care if it was weak or not, he simply wanted change; and change he *would* get if he embraced Reaping Icon. Change for the hell of it.

* * *

31

Christmas was always a tricky time in the Edwards household. Ruby didn't like the fact that she had to do all the work. She had to do all the work around here anyway, really, whether it was Christmas or not. Her husband Arthur, completely bald and fat now that he quickly passed sixty, had long said things would change around the place. But, they never changed for long. The only thing that was in constant change was the distance he had to sit from the table – his ever-enlarging stomach pushing him further and further away as it pressed up against it. Every argument that occurred between the couple would result in a bit of change on Arthur's part, for a bit, and then things would soon change back; flopping into their previous position like a river whose course people had tried to tinker with. Would that river heed to the thirsty demands of humanity? Would it hell. So, Arthur was that unending river, bursting his banks now and again when he was overcome with too much drink but forever going in the same direction. The grave was his only option, but he was taking his time getting there. Ruby slapped the turkey she'd just lovingly carved down on the table in front of her husband and dragged her sweaty, freckled hands through her thinning grey-ginger curls in despair as Arthur eyed its glaze, yawning. He grabbed some with his grubby fingers and dropped it on his plate, tossing a pile onto Alex's plate as well. Alex looked at Arthur's hands – mucky from playing around with the log burner and now oily from the turkey – then at the unused meat fork sitting next to the turkey. Alex didn't like Arthur. He didn't like Ruby either. At this moment in time, as he sat down for the annual Edwards Christmas dinner with a massive pile of meat and two veg slopped in front of him, he didn't like anyone. Arthur blew a party whistle right in Alex's face, who gritted his teeth as he stared at Katie – the only one around the table who wasn't wearing a paper hat. Alex felt like tearing his off and ramming it down somebody's throat, but he couldn't bring himself to do so... he couldn't find the will to do it. His whole body tensed and spasmed as he bared the howls and cackles from Arthur the clown next to him. On the other side sat Uncle Curly, Arthur's brother, who'd been drunk since well before lunch. He, his eyes more glazed than any turkey could ever hope to be, simply alternated between giggling to himself and sighing as he avoided engaging with the rest of the family. He wore his Christmas hat over his ever-fixed tweed flat cap, which hadn't been removed from his head in at least thirty years. He was, like Arthur, once a thin man but now beer-bellied and round-shouldered. Everybody had forgotten who the elder brother was, but it didn't really matter. They were close in age and similar in personality. Neither had gained authority over the other, both being equally ineffectual. Alex was only too glad that Uncle Curly had overdone it on the booze and was now incapable of joining in with Arthur's larking.

'Come on,' Ruby tried her best, flopping down on her chair and picking her glass of fizzy wine up. 'Merry Christmas.'

Curly downed his glass in one go, bursting into tears. 'Why did she leave me?' he sobbed uncontrollably, staring at the floor.

'Eat your dinner, Curly, it'll go cold otherwise,' Ruby told him.

'Yeah, shut up,' Arthur grunted, 'you fat fool.' He filled his mouth with a whole roast potato and carried on talking. 'She left you 'cause you're a fat slob,' he went on, spitting over Alex's dinner as he turned to look for the cranberry sauce.

Curly grabbed the bottle of fizz and filled his glass up, spilling some over his dinner.

A little later, after the sherry trifle had been well and truly polished off, the family settled down in front of the TV. Katie positioned herself as far away from Alex as she could, and he didn't argue with her. The Prime Minister came on, delivering his Christmas wishes:

'Today is a day to sit back and enjoy our time with our loved-ones.' Alex looked over at Katie as the PM continued: 'My family and I wish all of you out there a very merry Christmas, happy in the knowledge that the new year brings many great things for our country.'

'Bullshit,' Arthur called out, his paper hat sitting lopsided on his head. Ruby glared scornfully at him.

'The new year brings dignity to all those seeking it,' the PM went on. Arthur grabbed hold of the remote control and changed the channel.

'Oh what a wonderful time of year,' Curly started singing, waving a can of lager in front of his face, before collapsing in a heap on Alex's lap. Alex pushed him off and jumped up.

'I need some...' he announcing, some bizarre pain seizing his mind. It was a sensation he had never quite felt before. For some reason his mind was now full of The Space – not The Space in itself, but thoughts of It; like some Thing, some Being, had placed the thoughts there. 'I need some space,' he said, feeling he wasn't speaking his own words. He left the room.

* * *

Outside in the cold, Reaping Icon came to stand next to Alex. 'You need an aim in life,' said Reaping Icon, looking across the street at Emma's house. 'Something to give your existence meaning.'

'Like what?'

Reaping Icon tapped his chin, humming. 'Assassinate the Prime Minister?' he suggested casually. 'He's planning on being very naughty. You could stop him.'

'What? No, no, I'm not doing anything like that.'

'Why not – haven't you got it in you?'

A large black car pulled up at the end of the drive and, the engine still running, just waited there. Alex felt compelled to go to it, too nervous to challenge Reaping Icon. As he did, the back door opened and he looked inside. Sitting on the back seat was a fairly elderly man in a smart black pinstripe suit. His grey hair was slicked back with gel, and his teeth held between them a huge cigar. 'Get in,' the man said without moving his mouth, the sound escaping either side of the aromatic burning brown tube.

'Or you could rape your wife,' Reaping Icon whispered in Alex's ear. Alex got in the car and it drove off.

'Where are we going?' Alex asked the elderly gent, looking around inside the car. All he could see looking forward was his own reflection in a vast, bland metallic sheet shielding the driver.

'You have been invited to speak with the government,' he told Alex.

'Why me?'

'The Prime Minister asked for you specifically.'

'Really? Me?' Alex was quite pleased for a moment, suddenly remembering what Reaping Icon had just suggested to him. He dropped the conversation, remaining silent for the rest of the journey. His mind travelled from recess to recess, pondering over everything he'd done so far in his life. That shouldn't have taken too long, to be fair, as he'd not really done that much at all. He still worked in *Lennon's* shop – the only job he'd ever had since he was old enough to work and the only one he'd probably ever have – and his sham marriage was pitiful. He felt somehow that he deserved every piece of crap that got flung his way in life, simply because he hadn't put enough effort in to drag himself out of the cesspool. Still, it wasn't that bad. There were certainly people who were in a much worse mess than he was. He knew that he could, *could*, alter things if he really wanted to – if he *needed* to. Perhaps he was biding his time, he thought, for the right motivation to come along. Was that event now beginning to unfold as he sat in the back of this car on his way to the PM? Possibly. Time would tell, wouldn't it?

He checked his watch. It was an hour fast. He never did alter it when the clocks go back in the autumn – he liked to think he preferred to live in twelve months of summer time instead, and that not changing his watch would reflect this. The more likely reason was he was too idle to change it. It was a simple task, changing the time on a watch twice a year, but he chose not to. He had taken himself out of abiding by that rule – one of the only rules that he did bend, and one that had no consequence on others. What a shrivelled little turd it made him feel. Again he checked his watch, somehow hoping the hour had altered of its own accord. Katie had long picked at him for not changing the hour. One tiny victory against her was still a victory. Katie picked at everything he did. He caught his reflection in the metallic sheet in front, the paper hat out of the cracker still on his head. Katie must once have seen something in him, and he in her. That was over ten years ago now – a long time. Something made him feel they'd just settled for each other, thinking they could do no better. Clearly Katie had not confronted her true sexuality and allowed herself to get carried into a dead marriage. There was dead silence in the back of the car, and Alex could see the elderly man was smiling as he puffed on the cigar. It wasn't a particularly unpleasant smell, but Alex just wished he wasn't smoking. Somehow it made him feel the lesser of the two – or, at the very least, he attributed this feeling of inadequacy in comparison to his fellow occupant to the cigar. It stood between them, lying there in the man's mouth like a lead barrier or a gaping chasm. And, just like lead, its poison both swirled in plain sight and seeped in the unseen. Alex could see nothing at this exact point in time; he was at a loss to know what could be done to rectify anything that had befallen him. Yes, he could leave his wife and enter instead into a relationship with Emma, the one he should have been with all along; but somehow that seemed out of the question. Things never were that easy, were they? He just couldn't find the gumption within himself to take that extra bit of effort needed. Never mind, he was on his way to meet the PM for some reason, and perhaps that would sort everything out for him. His mere presence – being there whilst things unfolded around him – would be enough to spark alteration.

Several hours passed and Alex needed the toilet. He wanted to ask the man if he'd stop the car so that he could dive behind a bush and relieve himself, but he couldn't pluck up the courage. Then, they pulled into an underground car park and came to a halt. The elderly gent sat silently for a moment, gurning right at his young passenger, before checking his watch. 'Goodbye,' he said to Alex, and looked past him through the window. Alex turned to look, seeing nothing but an empty car park.

'What now?' he asked the gent nervously.

'Cigar?' he asked back, taking one from his inside jacket pocket.

'No, thanks.'

'This is where we part company,' he carried on, putting the cigar back in his pocket with a look of mild sadness on his face. He again looked past Alex and out of the window. Alex slowly opened the door and stepped out, closing the door again just in time for the car to speed off.

He looked bemusedly around the empty space, wondering to himself if he looked suspicious. He now desperately needed the toilet, but couldn't very well relieve himself here. Looking around, he saw a bright green exit sign up ahead in the distance, even though it was in the opposite direction the car had just gone in. He started to walk towards it, hands deep in his pockets, as the sound of an engine came back into his ears. He turned to see the same car speeding towards him. The brakes slammed on and the rear window opened. Expecting the elderly man, Alex instead saw the PM sitting in the back. 'Am I glad to see you!' he went, a look of dread on his face. Alex read his expression as relief, and felt instantly pleased and somehow important. The PM needed him! Oh, what splendour. 'Get in, get in!' he went on. Alex did so, getting back in the car and speeding off with the main man.

'What's this all about?' Alex asked him.

'My friend, you and I are going to make history,' he beamed with joy, and a hint of horror, 'we are going to change the world.'

'How'?

'You don't know who you are, do you?'

'I'm Alex.'

The PM smiled then frowned, deep in thought as his stare loomed deep into Alex's mystified gaze. 'I trust you've had words with Reaping Icon by now, in this current lifetime?'

'How do you know about Reaping Icon, and what do you mean this lifetime?'

'Alex!' the PM laughed, 'Reaping Icon has been in touch with me as well. We are both one of The Great Collective. You and I, some of the last few immortals... plagued by these false memories and endless life after life. Reaping Icon has promised to change all that, if we assist him.'

'Eh?' Alex was dumbfounded, barely able to form a glib response, let alone take any of the PM's words in. 'I thought I'd made him up in my mind, like an invisible friend or something.'

'An invisible friend?' the PM roared with laughter, clutching his stomach as the hilarity of such a thing stunned him with powerful physical guffaws. Suddenly, he was deadly still again with no trace of even a giggle as he turned to Alex with such pain and sorrow tearing at his self and whispered: 'He is anything but our friend.'

Alex studied closely the PM's shiny face; he couldn't help

it, it was so near to his own right now. It was so glossy, so over-produced just like it appeared on TV. This in itself felt strange to Alex as he'd always have expected it to be totally different to what the TV showed. Dry, grey and cracked would have been the reality Alex was expecting, but instead he got the moist smooth sheen as seen on the box. Not that it mattered, but there was something untoward about the PM's face – like it wasn't his actual face. Beneath the glitzy skin, worn soft and round like a pebble on the bed of a fast-flowing river, lay that dry, grey and cracked person Alex presumed he would physically see. He desperately needed the toilet.

'We have much to achieve using our connection to The Space, my immortal companion,' the PM continued. 'We will cure world hunger, end all wars… we will be supreme leaders of Earth!' He looked up to the heavens, obscured by the roof of the car, as Alex scratched his chin.

The two men made their way into the PM's office, where the main man closed and locked the door. Behind the vast oak desk, a green leather material covering its surface, stood a huge black upright box. It could have been a coffin stood on its end, but Alex couldn't see any removable lid. He did, however, feel keen about it in an uneasy way. It drew him in to have a look; kept wanting more and more attention as it just stood there.

'What's that?' Alex asked.

'That's my desk,' the PM replied in haste, smiling.

'No, the big box behind it,' Alex clarified.

The PM crept over to Alex, turning his back to the box and whispered: 'You've forgotten everything from your past existences, haven't you?'

'What past existences?'

The PM went over to the box and touched it, sighing, before sitting down at his desk in front of it. 'There are a small number of us left, Alex, who haven't been completely diluted by centuries of wiped memories. These few, we must trace; then, we start our work to bring the human race together as one force... an intergalactic force for good!'

'And what does that entail?'

'We must gather The Great Collective back together and ensure we remember from this life to the next. That way, we can sort this mess out on Earth and pool all our resources into heading for the stars.'

'And what's out there?'

'Humanity's future, of course. Listen, Alex, if we're going to be living forever then we must expand our horizons. Earth is tired, worn out. If we do not jump ship, head out and find new planets to live on, our subsequent lives will become increasingly horrific.' The PM held back tears as he saw in his spacely vision what lay in wait for the future of humanity – a future that was nearing at pace. 'First, it'll be too hot here, then... oh, the horrors!' He sobbed, waving his fists about at unseen enemies. Then, he stood up straight and caught his reflection in a large mirror across the room. Pointing at his own face, he yelled: 'I'm watching you, fucker!' Sitting back down with intent, he picked up two pencils off his desk and sharpened them furiously. 'I don't know if I can go on, Alex, in this current life. Mark my words, though, I will be back and we will continue our plans.' So intense was his desire not to exist at this exact moment in time that he stuck the sharpened pencils up his nostrils and yelled, 'Long live The Great Collective,' before bashing his head down on the desk, driving the pencils deep up his nose and into his brain and ending its ability to function. Blood oozed out of his face as he lifted it up off the desk and looked over at Alex looking back in terror. 'It hurts,' he mumbled, before his face slammed back onto the desk. Bye, bye, PM. Alex looked over at the mirror, the paper hat sitting on his head like a vivid release of obnoxious innocence. Things felt very wet between his legs, and he looked down to see that he'd wet himself. There came a knock at the door. Alex froze, deadly silent, keeping his eyes on himself in the mirror. Just a couple of hours ago he'd been sitting with his wife and the in-laws having Christmas dinner; now he was locked in the PM's office with the dead body of the main man. His enjoyment of Christmas had been dwindling fairly steadily year after year since he'd left childhood, and this was now perhaps one of the worst. At least it was different, though. He imagined himself off somewhere else on an amazing adventure with thrills and spills hitherto unexperienced. He had hardly experienced anything yet in his short life, so these thrills and spills needn't have been too extravagant. His imagination was not the most waxing and he quickly found himself backed into a corner and confined to his present predicament. He wanted to do things in his life, yes, it's just that he hadn't really given much thought as to what things. He wanted to be with Emma, and yet he didn't. It was a muddle, a hotchpotch of gobbledygook mashing around his mush-brain. He'd continued with Katie just that little bit too long, and felt he couldn't come out of it now. Would he lose face? Would he regret leaving Katie?

The knock came again at the door, and to Alex it felt like a knock to the head. It shook him out of his daydream and the only thing for him to do was go to the door, unlock it and let the person in. He could have committed suicide instead, but it didn't cross his mind.

* * *

'That's how I ended up in here,' Alex told Noose, staring at the metal struts holding the top bunk that housed his roommate.

'Yes, it's awkward when something like that happens,' was Noose's lazy reply. He hadn't really been listening; he was still staring up at that face on the cell ceiling. It was now everything to him – his one big obsession. Focus on it could possibly see him occupied throughout his lengthy prison term, or it would drive him over the edge into nonreturnable madness. Perhaps it was already too late.

'At least I know who set me up,' Alex carried on in spite of Noose's lack of interest. Noose did not respond. 'Reaping Icon, that's who.'

Just now the cell door opened and three very large bald prisoners came in, followed by an extremely thin, pale young prisoner. Noose didn't acknowledge their arrival, but instinctively knew there was trouble ahead.

'Get down,' the wispy man ordered Noose. He obliged, getting off the bunk and facing the four men. Alex was frozen in terror, selfishly hoping it was just Noose they had come for. Noose kind of knew what it was about, as he'd heard Wayne Richards had been transferred to this prison. He was the father of Beth Henderson; the man who had once presumably been romantically connected with Dani Henderson in order to father the poor child. Both were dead, and to all intents and purposes Noose was responsible. 'You know who I am, don't you?' Richards spat at Noose. He nodded back.

'For what it's worth, I was framed for their murders,' Noose uttered. For this, Richards head-butted him. Noose did not flinch, though he now had a bloodied nose.

'You,' Richards addressed Alex, 'strip.'

Two of the huge men now took hold of Noose as the third closed the cell door and grabbed hold of Alex. The young man, limp in the big man's grip, looked over at Noose.

'Do it,' Noose sighed, looking away.

'No, no, fuck you, fuck you all,' Alex cried. 'Help, guards!' he yelled. The big man smacked him across the face and started tearing his clothes off.

Richards turned to Noose and smiled as he took his own clothes off. It was a struggle, but the big man managed to strip

Alex, punching him numerous times in the face in order to succeed. Richards rubbed his own naked body up and down, his penis erecting as he knelt on the bed next to Alex. 'Shush, my lover, it's futile to fight our burning attraction,' Richards cooed in his ear as the big man spun Alex onto his stomach. He sensually rubbed Alex's body up and down from on top of him, leaning over and kissing him on the neck. Alex sobbed and sobbed as he felt Richards' penis enter from behind. Deeper and deeper it went, in and out and in and out. Faster, harder, it got; the pain and indignity so overwhelming that he imagined himself deep underground, burning and suffocating to death. Finally, he passed out as the two men holding Noose forced him to his knees and Richards pulled out of Alex and turned to Noose with his penis in-hand, ejaculating over his face. 'Give it a kiss,' Richards demanded, the two men pulling Noose's head back as the penis entered his mouth. Noose sucked the last of the sperm, blood and poo off the penis as Richards slowly pulled it out. Then, he nodded and all three men began thrashing the hell out of the poor bastard as he tried to protect his face. Richards sat back down on the bottom bunk with the unconscious Alex, running his fingers through the young man's hair.

When all is said and done
He has simply forgotten to come.
What are you left with?
Pure masses of fable and fantastic,
Gracefully perceiving to unrest and deny?

And so…

THE WAITING ROOM

Noose was sitting in the bright white waiting room, twiddling his thumbs. The magazines on the table in the centre of the room didn't really take his fancy. Instead, he thought about being dead and that this was his turn to find out where his leftover essence would end up. Then, the door opposite opened and Peter Smith strolled in. Wearing his father's lovingly tailored old brown suit, he sat down across from Noose and smiled.

'Am I glad to see you,' Noose said calmly, and a little unsurprised. 'So it's true, I *am* dead.' He sounded rather relieved.

'Not quite, Noose,' Peter replied. 'Well, at this exact moment in time you are dead, yes, but the doctors and nurses are trying their best on you and you should pull through. A bit of resuscitation and you'll be fine.'

'Ah, I see.'

'Yes. Marvellous really, isn't it?'

'That they can bring people back from the dead?'

'No – that doctors and nurses will tirelessly work their socks off to save a convicted child rapist and murderer.'

'I didn't do it,' Noose shouted angrily, getting up from his chair. He paced up and down, livid with the turn of events in his life of late.

'I know you didn't, but they don't.'

'Then who did? Who set me up?' Noose demanded, grabbing Peter and pulling him to his feet. 'If you're up here watching down on everything, you must have seen it happen.'

'Up here? Must I be looking down... or even up? Noose,' Peter carried on, pulling himself gently away from the angry man. 'I am right next to you at all times, right next to everyone. It only takes a mere step to the side to get here.'

'What's it all about, anyway? I mean, you're long dead, how can I be talking to you right now? Is it really you?'

'I have assumed this bodily form as it is the one you most readily associate with me.'

'What do you mean by that?'

'I am one of The Great Collective,' Peter explained with some sadness, 'an Icon who has been scattered and fragmented across all of time.'

'The Great Collective?'

'We were the first people on Earth, hundreds of years ago, to discover and make contact with The Space – the summation of all that ever was, is or will be. We planned such greatness and good with our new aid. The Space granted us immortality for our efforts.'

'Ah, I see,' Noose yawned, sitting back down and rubbing his chin.

'However,' Peter continued, 'it was a sick curse – immortality with the added kick of dying after each lifespan and being reborn as somebody else. Each time we were reborn we lost our memory, and would struggle to reform our connection to The Space. Our power to contact The Space ebbed. As we grew collectively weaker, so the evil within us separated and became its own entity – Reaping Icon.'

'Reaping Icon?' Noose searched his mind for a fleeting memory of that name. He had certainly heard it before.

'Reaping Icon was the first to harness The Space for ill. It was this revelation that brought about the sheer *need* to collectively remember. Reaping Icon *must* be stopped. The more we forget, the more powerful he grows.'

'But your family, your life here on Earth? What about all that?' Noose asked, beginning to take this seriously.

'I *am* Peter Smith, yes, and all of that has happened and will continue to happen. But, I have also been other people, other Peter Smith's, and led so many other lives. However, currently I am forever trapped in an unending cycle of this single lifespan, replaying it over and over again with slight alterations.'

'You have been other people in the past?' Noose questioned, almost like he was asking himself. He couldn't get his head around it.

'Countless others, throughout history.'

'And you will go on being other people?'

'I hope not. If The Space remains closed, then no. In my conscious ignorance my sub-conscious had closed The Space, but Reaping Icon has worked cracks open, intent on continuing this sickness for the hell of it. There are others, also, who wish for The Space to be fully open in order to grasp infinite knowledge and immortality.'

'Why are you trapped as Peter Smith then?' Noose asked, trying to take it all in his stride. Part of him felt he was having a very bad dream, and he was willing to ride it out until he wakened.

'The Space is the great balancer of things – if everything is not perfectly so, then it will not allow us to move on. That Lucy's death is still attached to Peter, to me, is the bind. I must discover her killer and put things right.'

'Why won't The Space just tell you who murdered her if it is this all-powerful thing?' Noose reasoned.

'If only it was that easy. Oh how I have begged The Space to tell me,' Peter cried.

'Maybe Reaping Icon murdered her?'

'No. I know all the evil Reaping Icon commits in my name – it is instantly etched in my own mind as though I have done it with my own hands. He is, after all, the darkness within all of The Great Collective. He is all of us, he is me.'

'That's monstrous.'

'I am the final link between The Great Collective and The Space, the last of us who can still actively harness The Space's power. There is too much dilution of memory between the others. It all rests on me, unless Reaping Icon has his way and succeeds with his current scheme.'

'Well what can you do, if you're dead?' Noose questioned, confused.

'There is very little I can do from here, trapped by the might of Reaping Icon. We must keep this current cycle flowing, try to fix things now and not let it undo itself and play over yet again.' Peter put his head in his hands. 'I am so tired of re-living this life over and over again.' He walked away from Noose. 'Yes, my suicide was a mistake, but I had become too encompassed and overwhelmed with this sordid life. My connection to The Space has truly been a sick curse. You see all of good, and also ultimately all of evil – it is too much to bear; it sickens you, warps your mind. I am forever tainted, my worldview stunted and twisted towards the cruel.' He turned back to Noose. 'You yourself said that I was capable of such good, and yet I ended up doing such sick things again and again. Whilst I continue to live this immortal curse, I will continue to fall down like that.'

'There *is* terrible cruelty and suffering in the world, yes,' Noose responded, 'but there is also the possibly and the hope for amazing wonders.'

'Nature is a wonder; a wonder of survival. All survival boils down to is killing something weaker than yourself. Life, hah! Life is but an opportunity to cause pain and death for others. What is the circle of life, but a sick joke on endless repeat?'

'Then why bother at all, why do anything?'

'Because there *is* that chance, that ever so slim chance, of putting things right at the very last moment and achieving something truly amazing.' Peter smiled, but it was a sad smile full of sorrow and regret. 'You must seek out who murdered those poor people and framed you, it is your call and only yours. The truth is locked away deep in the mind of the true killer, and only you can find them.'

'Why can't The Space help?'

'The Space is the summation of everything that was, is, or will be; but it is for each of us to try to harness and gain access to this. It is not an open book or a big man in the sky waiting to answer our prayers.'

'But how can I gain access to it?' Noose pleaded, seeing a chance to clear his name and trying desperately to seize it.

'You cannot, you must fall back on your own humanity to solve it. And, I must ask you a favour: I implore you to seek out and make contact with the keepers of The Space. There is some good left in the ones who are not dead.'

'The keepers of The Space? Where can I find them?'

'They once masqueraded as the Museum Club – the secret gathering of minds that took me on and re-introduced me to The Space in this lifespan. They were unable to keep contact with The Space for long, so needed me. Reaping Icon was too strong, turning them into murderers and blocking my mind again and again.'

'There were those murders by Barbara Davies at the museum: Louis Sellers and James Harrington, all those years ago,' Noose remembered, searching his mind. 'And then there was the murder of those other three men afterwards, deep in the museum, like a sacrifice of some sort. We never did identify those men.'

'They were some of the keepers of The Space, driven to madness and ultimately their own deaths.'

'So some are still alive, and you want me to seek them out? It's crazy!' Noose laughed.

'Yes, you must. It is the only way I can put things right and try to end Reaping Icon's reign of horror.'

'Well what do I do when I find them?'

'You will know what to do,' was Peter's simple reply. Noose wasn't so sure he *would* know what to do.

'Yes, I remember the murder of those three men – you were so young and innocent, Peter,' Noose saw back in his mind. 'Corrupted by these intrusions into your life, you didn't stand a chance did you? Then,' Noose welled-up, 'then there was Lucy.'

'The worst thing I could ever have done was forget her,' Peter lamented, trying to keep his demeanour balanced so as not to upset Noose further. 'But, I did. My mind was quick to wipe itself away each time, egged-on by Reaping Icon's ceaseless shadow-attacks.'

'Did the keepers of The Space murder her?' Noose wondered, clenching his fists and looking ready to murder someone himself.

'They would never have done that to me, would they? Even so, they *did* know who Lauren really is and did not at all want my connection with Lucy.'

'Lauren? What do you mean, who she really is?' But, Noose began to fade, feeling himself pulled away from this space. Strangely, he wanted to stay – he felt at home in Peter's company. If this *was* Peter.

'There is very little time left,' Peter whispered, moving and sitting back next to Noose and leaning in close. 'You, Noose, are not one of The Great Collective, but you can help set me free. All I want is to live and die like a normal man, like I should have done from the start. This current lifespan as Peter Smith is my last chance. For this, Reaping Icon must be stopped.'

'What can I do?'

'Alex; he is one, and Reaping Icon has made contact. You must do all you can to stop him from realising his full connection to The Space. If Reaping Icon can harness Alex's forgotten residual connection, I will no longer be the final link and there will be terrible suffering.'

Noose suddenly wakened in hospital, two armed police officers standing either side of his bed as Inspector Nicola Williams hovered over him.

'Oh God, Henry,' she spoke lightly, holding his handcuffed hand, 'what a mess we're in.'

'Peter,' he coughed.

'Peter? Peter Smith? He's dead, Henry, Peter Smith is dead.'

'I saw him,' Noose went on, trying to sit up. His body, and the handcuffs keeping him attached to the bed, would not allow it.

'Of course you did,' Williams comforted him, rolling her eyes. 'Listen, you nearly died in prison. It's not safe for a child sex criminal in there, we're trying to get you put into maximum security solitary confinement.' She smiled encouragingly, squeezing his hand.

'I'm innocent, for fuck sake,' he growled, digging his nails into her hand. She recoiled, the two officers on guard stepping forward.

'I'm fine,' she said to them, grabbing hold of Noose's hand again. 'Listen to me,' she said, pressing something into Noose's palm, 'you were found guilty in a court of law, so that's that.' She stared intently into his eyes, he momentarily flicking his to the guards. 'There is no escape, no re-trial; just a hard slog.' She leant in close, kissing him on the forehead. 'I did have feelings for you, once,' she uttered, before kissing him again. Then, she let go and walked away, without turning to look back. Noose gripped his hand; he knew it was the key for the handcuffs. But why? Why would Williams want to help him escape? Did he even want to escape? That would make him a fugitive, a guilty murderer on the loose forever hunted down. Anything was better than going back to prison, he supposed. And, as his memory of talking to Peter just now quickly faded like a muddy dream, he kept thinking about the museum club. Suddenly he could remember nothing but the museum club, and thought perhaps it was a clue from either Peter or his subconscious about the one who had framed him. He clenched the key, looking up at the armed officers, and wondered what to do next. He felt as rough as toast right now; there wasn't a lot he could do.

The ills that men do put upon
Their own shoulders.
Yet we seek out greater meaning,
Shoulders of giants.

Piling on the ill intentions,
Corrupting our own children.
Praying to a higher Man,
His shoulders weighted with burden.

WHAT HAPPENED TO ALEX NEXT

Alex sat and waited for his visitor to arrive. He'd had very few people come to see him in prison so far; few people who he knew. Being the man convicted of murdering the Prime Minister, he had had quite a bit of media exposure and was routinely being asked for interviews and generally receiving fan mail from extremists and the like. He didn't like all that, and so far had managed to curb his derailment into that area. His legal aides were advising that there was plenty of time for all that, anyway, and he was best to bide his time before he "sold his story" in order to get the best deal. Being married to the woman whose family once harboured Peter Smith, as well, didn't ease the attention he'd received. One person who certainly hadn't visited him in prison was his wife. There had been no sign of Katie or the rest of her family, and even visits from his own family had been thin on the ground. Still, he'd always seen himself as an orphan who had never had a real belonging. There had been an extended stay with one foster family, with whom he'd grown quite attached, but this came to a natural end when he started going out with Katie and her family sort of took him on. He wasn't really upset or concerned by his lack of a biological belonging, but owing to his current situation it might have helped him through a bit. The media, of course, had made much of his family background. Still, this wasn't at all his most pressing concern right now; the fact he'd been anally raped *was* pretty high on his list of upsets, though. The perpetrator had received a rap over the knuckles, but little more. If anything, Alex perceived that the authorities had somehow turned a blind eye at the time and let it happen. The guards were certainly greeting him with smirks and winks now – at least, that's what he saw. He felt about as low as he could, knowing he'd never been this down in all his life. He thought he'd had a hard life before all this happened to him, now he knew it had been a breeze.

There was no breeze in the room where he was currently sitting. He looked around at his fellow prisoners, some embracing their loved-ones whilst others tried to keep up a front and an arrogant distance with their visitor. He wondered how he should greet and act with his. There was nobody but himself willing to give an answer, and even then he didn't know whether or not to rely on his own decision. Decisions hadn't been his strongpoint in a long time, if ever, and Reaping Icon didn't seem to want to help. There had been no sign of Reaping Icon.

Emma walked in and looked nervously around before spotting Alex. He wanted to stand up to greet her as she rushed over, but the pain in his backside was still so intense as to dissuade him from sudden movements. She sat down across from him as an inmate gave her a wolf-whistle. Alex thought how utterly gorgeous she had become in the passing years. Here, in her late twenties, she was even more appealing than she'd been as a teenager, and he completely regretted ever letting things get so far with Katie. She took his hand and gripped it tightly, her hair darker than it had ever been and her skin crying out for a glimpse of the sun.

'I'm sorry I haven't been before now,' she said, looking down.

'Thank you for coming at all,' he replied, almost whispering, as he looked around the room for potential eavesdroppers. 'I thought I'd never see you again.'

'I can't quite believe what's happened, it's all so crazy.' Now she looked up, and it was Alex's turn to look away. 'One day the papers are painting you as a monster, the next you're a hero.'

'I'm neither. I didn't do it,' Alex mumbled, tired of repeating himself.

'You were definitely set up, that's agreed by everyone,' Emma replied, squeezing his hand. He looked up and their eyes met.

'Everyone thinks I'm innocent?'

'Well, yeah, most people.'

He pulled his hand from hers. 'What about Katie?'

'I always wondered why you married her, Alex; why you walked headlong into a disaster you could clearly see coming.'

'And what were your conclusions?'

'That you are weak,' she said bluntly, trying to deliver it with a smile but failing.

'Thanks.'

'And,' she carried on, calmly but assuredly, 'I kinda know that you and I wouldn't have worked out either, because you're just not enough of a man.'

'Is that why I married a lesbian, then?' Alex sighed, his last grasp of human connection slipping away as he received Emma's character assassination. She gave out a little cough as he rubbed his sore eyes. 'Back then, we were just kids. I didn't think I stood a chance with you, you were the most amazing girl in school. I blocked any thoughts of you and me from my mind. It was a simple no-no.'

'Even after I told you how I felt?' she came back at him, holding back the tears.

'Katie, she was in a bad place; I felt I couldn't step away from her. I don't know, Emma, I just don't know anything. I'm a complete useless turd.'

She grabbed his hand again and they sat there silently for a time, neither knowing what to say.

Emma eventually broke the silence with: 'The only men I seem to get sniffing around me are dickheads. They're all just after one thing, and they can't see past my looks. I guess that's why I wanted you, because you didn't show any interest in me in that way.'

'All I've ever seen in girls are their looks. If I rated their looks too highly, I didn't bother with them… not that I bothered much with girls. Remember how long it took me to get together with Katie? That was vomit-inducing stuff.'

'Look, there's a life outside of here, but it's not with Katie.'

'I don't want Katie. I want you, Emma.'

'I don't know if we could have something together, Alex,' she cut. 'But, there *is* something. I don't understand it, but I guess I'm here now aren't I?'

'I need to stand up, I know, and stop being this weak and feeble little piece of snot. I will try to be the man you want me to be. Please, Emma,' he grasped her hand tighter and tighter, a sensation of pins and needles running through it. 'Everyone else has ditched me but you.'

The bell had gone, visitors were being cleared out. 'I must go,' she cried, the tears bursting like bullets from their ducts as she pulled away to go. 'I'll come back, I promise.'

With this promise, and possible future beyond his current stupor, Alex felt a rush of joy and renewed vigour drawn into his body. The crushing on his chest leapt away and he watched in awe as its visual embodiment as a grey mist evaporated. His eyes lost the last image of Emma as she disappeared from the room and he turned to leave in the opposite direction. As he did so, he bumped into a familiar face.

'You lucky man,' said Reaping Icon. 'I came back just in the nick of time.'

'Go away, I don't want you interfering with me.'

'That's gratitude,' Reaping Icon laughed, stalking behind Alex as he was marched off back to his cell.

Back in the cell, Reaping Icon appeared the other side of the door and said: 'I can get you out of here.'

'Go away,' Alex said again, tossing and turning on the bed.

'Oh don't be silly, now. Listen, all you have to do is concentrate really hard and The Space will grant you whatever you so wish. You could walk straight out of here unimpeded.'

'And what then? Once I'm out, would I just magically be allowed to stay out for the rest of my life? Of course not!'

'The Space can grant you that which you most desire. Emma, for instance, will be putty in your hands.'

'I don't want her to be putty in my hands.'

Reaping Icon now appeared in the cell and strolled around quite amply, as if the room was much vaster than it appeared to Alex. 'Open your mind, placate the sensual! Do not let the undiluted remain as such,' he said.

'You're talking gibberish.'

'Alex, Alex! Your mind is so closed to that which it once harnessed. You are one of The Great Collective, a towering immortal who once ruled almighty over all of existence. Your connection to The Space allowed endless pleasure and knowledge; do not let your current self forget that.' And now, Reaping Icon looked behind Alex. But, he would not turn to look at what Reaping Icon could see. 'It is coming, It is almost with us in spite of Its closing at the hands of Peter Smith. Ease your resistance, Alex, It is The Space as controlled by me – by Us!'

For the first time since Reaping Icon's presence in his life, Alex felt an inseparable bond with him and could not clear his mind of the man. If he *was* a man. He seemed both a man *and* everything else that was not a man – just what Alex equally thought of himself. He could feel Reaping Icon drawing closer and closer, fulfilling a dreadful ageless bond as they united in mind. Reaping Icon had come from him, just as he had come from all of The Great Collective, but now he returned singularly to Alex. He, and he alone, now had to contend with

Reaping Icon. No longer was Reaping Icon playing around in his training ground and requesting the pitiful damaged beings he had done for his games; he was enacting his ultimate desire and returning to bodily form with Alex as the host. He consumed Alex's mind, gushing freely into it like a vast storm rushing into an exposed cavernous recess. Alex was completely free from fight, completely free from the undiluted strength of his original self so many generations ago. They, as united discoverers of The Space, had played supreme with their bestowed gifts. But, to what avail? The Great Collective had been delivered the tragedy of self-renewing immortality and that endless cursed cycle of complete re-birth. It had taken away the desire to exist, because they knew they always *would* exist. More and more angry and confused had they become with their battle to remember their prior lives, that the manifestation of this growing hatred for life itself had now returned and decided upon bodily form. Reaping Icon, seizing Alex's shell as his own, casting aside all those memories of the immediate life Alex was living, was here to destroy all of Life itself. And, The Space had created all of this – It had given The Great Collective the sickness of eternal re-birth, an eternal roundabout of loss. Reaping Icon was everybody, and everybody was he – he was the summation of humanity, just as when he'd embodied poor Darren Aubrey as the Judge or thrown Peter Smith into the depths of depravity. That all the hate, all the pain, could so easily come to fruition and take Alex right now was testament to Life's wicked and ceaseless routine. There had been no end to the cruelty since existence had been sparked, and to all intents and purposes it now appeared as though Life would get its just desserts. Reaping Icon was the end result of The Space's opening up to humanity, and the ugly conclusion was no surprise. The Great Collective had treated The Space's "gift" as a sick, sick travesty, and the shit had most certainly hit the fan.

Alex focused his mind on the guard who had just locked his cell door, drawing him back. He returned, his whole self completely at Alex's mercy as he unlocked and opened the door, standing aside for Alex to stroll out. 'Take me to Wayne Richards,' he said to the guard.

Richards just laughed and stayed sitting when his cell door opened and Alex stepped in.

'Hey, honey,' Alex cooed, coming straight to Richards and placing his hand on the top of his head. The rapist convulsed and choked in agony and terror as Alex kept watch from above, his hand drawing all the life out. There wasn't much life to speak of, but Alex nonetheless wanted to take it away from the vile little shit. And soon enough he had his wish, lifting his hand away and letting the corpse drop to the floor like an over-ripe gooseberry.

Alex stepped back and looked down at what he'd done. He couldn't quite believe it, as though it had happened in a dream away from his conscious control. Not really worried by his actions, he turned and walked out as the cell door was once again shut and locked.

Technology outstripping morality,
A Pandora's box of devils
Unleashed.

Nature endlessly self-replenishing,
Trundling, trundling along
Endlessly.

WHAT HAPPENED
TO NOOSE NEXT

(PART ONE)

Noose couldn't see the face on the carpet from his hospital bed, but he knew it was there. He could just sense that he was being watched. Only one guard was currently in place, and he wasn't looking at Noose. If anything, he was looking down at the floor. Was the floor carpeted? Being a hospital ward, probably not; but Noose just *knew* that the face was down there looking up. Why wasn't it on the ceiling where he could keep an eye on it? The face was being rather cunning, he thought, and evading him. What was it up to?

The guard gave out a little yawn and checked his watch. Sorry to be keeping you up, Noose thought. He dare not have said it out loud. No, this whole situation had crushed his interaction with others to not much more than a responding to questions basis. It didn't do to enter into any kind of jocular retorting with the guard. In many ways this was what he missed most about Peter Smith – they had been such good verbal sparring partners. The same could have been said about Sergeant Stephen Noble too, but that had also ended in misery. Still, Noose was alive and this was perhaps his last hope at somehow coming up trumps in the end. Being alive afforded him at least the most minute smidgen of opportunity to put right what had occurred. With the key to the handcuffs in the palm of his hand, he needed only to wait for some strength to return before he could mount an escape bid.

Right this second a figure swept in, cloaked from head to toe in a creamy silk garment, their face shielded by a heavy hood. They held up a small device to the guard's neck, who promptly dropped to the floor unconscious. Two more hooded figures followed, all three standing over Noose's bed. 'Everything is nothing. No order, no lies,' they droned in unison. 'Deny your anchor, scape the goats. Everything is nothing. No boundaries, no battles.' One moved closer, pressing the device against Noose's neck.

* * *

'Have you been attentive?' Peter Smith asked. Noose opened his eyes and looked around, but he couldn't see where the voice was coming from. 'Have you been paying attention?'

'Peter, is that you?' Noose replied in desperation, seeing that he was the only person in the room. He was lying flat on a hard metallic slab, free from binds but still cursed by weakness following the attack in the prison. All around him were bumpy brown walls of earth, the damp musty smell of the moist air almost choking the poor man. He struggled into a sitting position, rubbing at his neck. 'Where are you?' he called out again to Peter, but there was no reply. Peter was dead, and that was that.

Noose stayed sitting in the same spot for quite a while, in some way glad he was no longer shackled to a hospital bed but in another way concerned about his current location. He'd become a man who was put in places, and taken about under the control of others. He had always been the one doing that before, so it kind of irritated him to have the tables turned. Anywhere was better than prison, though, so he quickly accepted the fact that the hooded figures had rescued him. It briefly crossed his mind that it may not have been a rescue at all, and that what might happen to him next could be so much worse than what had happened in prison. If that was possible.

'Everything is nothing. No order, no lies.'

Noose turned to see that the three figures were standing behind him, their faces constantly hidden. 'Who are you?' he asked them, getting to his feet. It was a struggle, the pain in his chest severe, but he tried to mask it. 'Why did you rescue me?'

'Henry Noose, the confidante of the final link,' they whispered together.

'I see,' Noose sighed. 'That makes a whole load of fucking sense, doesn't it!'

'Peter Smith! You are his current chosen corporeal companion.'

'Nice bit of alliteration there,' Noose replied glibly, clasping onto the metallic slab as he moved closer to them.

'He has chosen you as his anchor to humanity, you carry him with you.'

Noose sensed something, turning around to be confronted by the huge black upright box. It stood there, as silent as the vast emptiness of Noose's hope in humanity. 'Jeez Louise, does everything just appear in this blasted room?' He felt drawn to it, desperate to become it for some inexplicable reason. He could not turn away, wanting to let his body and mind be taken away from everything.

'Everything is nothing. No order, no lies. Deny your anchor, scape the goats. Everything is nothing. No boundaries, no battles,' they again chanted as Noose dropped to his knees, the tearing at his chest from within intensifying. 'Peter Smith. Our last chance. The final link. The final link between The Great Collective and The Space. He, and only he, can restore that which has passed.'

'What is all this?' Noose cried out, a screaming emanating

from deep inside his mind. Then, all at once it lifted, and he felt emptied of anguish. Possessed with renewed energy, he jumped to his feet and turned his back on the box.

'Peter, you must re-open The Space,' the hooded figures called out.

'Forever alive, the endless curse of existence,' a familiar voice replied. Noose slowly turned around again to face the box. It was gone, and in its place stood Peter Smith. 'There's no such thing as resting in peace.'

'No,' Noose wept, looking upon his once-dead friend. 'It's, it's not real. You died, you're dead.'

'Right now to the world, yet again, I was never dead. The universe has been tweaked once more. You are in the centre of my return this time, Noose – your timeline has not been adjusted accordingly.'

'I see,' Noose stoically responded, unable to remove his eyes from Peter's. Still, he was not unable to believe Peter had returned from the dead; he'd always felt there was something special about the man. And then, as he thought that, he instantly pitied Peter for not being allowed to remain dead. It felt like a terrible weakness. 'There's no such thing as resting in peace?'

'Peter, you must re-open The Space,' the hooded figures repeated. 'We have saved your companion from his fate and delivered you back to your human body so that you may complete your business.'

'My business? It's not *my* business to re-open The Space. It has been nothing but a sick, sick curse.'

'Reaping Icon has returned to bodily form, and only with The Space's assistance can he be defeated.'

'And you expect The Space to just play ball?'

'There is no other option.'

'Let Reaping Icon destroy all of Life…' Peter spat back.

'We are the keepers of The Space,' they carried on. 'We are

the ones entrusted to ensure the bond between humanity and The Space continues – it is ultimately the only way our species will survive beyond the end of the universe.'

Peter tutted, shaking his head. 'You entrusted yourselves.' He turned his back on them, rubbing his hand against the earthen wall and sniffing his fingers. 'Humanity doesn't deserve to survive. They can all go fuck themselves.' Peter turned back to the gathering, seeing that Noose was still entranced by his re-emergence into existence. 'Too much water has gone under the bridge to make a difference now.'

'Re-open The Space, defeat Reaping Icon, and you will be able to live, love and die like a normal person.'

'Free from my warped worldview? I think not. There's nothing normal about me; I'm a sick, pathetic excuse for Life just like the rest of you.'

'No,' Noose quickly interjected, 'that's bullshit. Whatever you've done, for whatever reason, there is *always* the hope of good coming from it.'

'You believe that about me,' Peter replied, placing his hand on Noose's shoulder. 'But, you simply don't believe it about yourself.'

'We're just human, Peter,' Noose grappled, taking Peter's hand. 'We're animals still evolving, still making mistakes. Surely there is the potential for something truly remarkable to come from us as a species?'

Peter looked deep into Noose and died a little again. He didn't want to hear any of this, he just wanted to keep on thinking the way he did. It was easier to keep thinking the same way. 'My mind is warped by what's happened to me and those around me, I must try to see through that,' he decided, holding onto Noose for dear life. This man had never, *never*, completely turned his back on him. Peter had had so many other lives before this one, but never had he come across a companion such as Noose. He knew now he loved the man, and for that reason felt whole and completed in his journey of life. This lasted for but a second, as thoughts of Lucy flooded his mind once more. She was gone, taken away by the ultimate sickness in humanity: murder. Though he wanted to end the cycle of murder gripping humanity, he also wanted to punish Lucy's killer with the same fate. That juxtaposition made him as human as everyone else, and it was for this reason that he most wanted to see an ultimate end for all. There was no special reason why The Space should grant him immortality, surely? It was all just meaningless in the end, and he didn't want to be around to suffer endlessness. 'The Museum Club,' Peter uttered, looking across at the hooded figures with a wry grin on his face. 'The power to draw me back from the waiting room, but powerless to stop Reaping Icon.'

'You are the final link. You, and only you, are undiluted enough to make the connection needed,' they answered together.

'Always hiding down your damp holes, aren't you,' Peter carried on at them with venom. 'I might have blocked it from my mind all those years ago, but I remember everything now.' Silently they stood, listening to The Peter Smith. 'I remember perfectly well what you did...'

The Pilgrim's staff is on the window sill,
Singing softly, it cannot be ill.
It's not real, it doesn't breathe,
It cannot affect you, or so you believe.

Hit across the head, the Pilgrim's dead,
Destroyed by the only thing he kept by his side.
It's a burdon – a burden
He must carry to his grave.

PETER JOINS THE MUSEUM CLUB

It was the day after I'd solved the murders of Louis Sellers and James Harrington at the museum. Barbara Davies was well on her way to a long stint in prison, and I felt compelled to return to the museum. I don't know why, as I always try not to get myself involved in things. But, on this occasion I walked straight in and discovered a meeting of the museum club was in progress. I could hear the voices pulsating from the room, though not exactly what they were saying. As I tried the door, I discovered it was locked. Quickly I turned and walked away, only to hear the sound of the door unlocking. I stopped and turned to see a man's face poking out. 'Peter Smith,' he spoke gently.

'Yes. How do you know who I am?'

'We've been expecting you.'

'Who has?'

'The museum club.'

'Oh. And who are you?'

'You will never know my name, nor the names of the other members.'

'That puts me at a disadvantage.'

'On the contrary.'

'I know the names of two members already… past members – Louis Sellers and James Harrington.'

He laughed. 'They were not members of *our* museum club. Come, join us. We have much to discuss.'

I went inside. There I found six figures standing with their backs to me, in long silk gowns and their heads covered in hoods. The unsheathed man who'd beckoned me in was bland and colourless, an unremarkable face sporting nothing but an excitable mouth which seemed to moisten as he watched me take in what my eyes were seeing. The room, too, was colourless and dull, empty but for the huge upright box.

'Who are you, what do you want?' I asked naively.

'My part has been played,' the man said, 'and now I must go.' He stepped up to the box, opening his arms out as though he was waiting to embrace a long-lost loved-one who was racing towards him from the distance. He dropped to his knees, his black hair turning instantly grey and falling out. I tried to pass the six hooded figures to go to him, but together they simply stopped me without a touch or a word spoken, and from what I could see of the man's crowd-face, it became awash with deep wrinkles and blotches of flaky red skin. 'Cease not,' were his final words, before his body slammed down onto the floor.

'He's dead,' I yelled, still unable to move to – or even away from – him.

'He is not dead, he has merely delivered himself back to the waiting room,' they told me in their eerie way. 'We are the keepers of The Space, and you are the final link between The Great Collective and The Space.'

'Come again?' I said, completely overwhelmed with what I'd just witnessed. I couldn't quite work out whether it had been real or some illusion. My mind was numbed to the sights and sounds of false horror from watching TV with Mother, that I now wondered if I could tell apart truth from reality.

'We too carry some residual essence from past lives, but it is miniscule. No longer can we rightly claim to be part of The Great Collective. But you, Peter Smith, are near complete as can be after so many years and lives.'

'Show me your faces, let me see you,' I demanded of them, mentally fighting their touch-less bonds.

'It is best you do not see our faces.'

'You must show me something,' I told them, trying to make some sense of all this. Strangely, though, it did feel familiar; I was not confused beyond return. Throughout my entire short life so far, I had felt some kind of block – some kind of impenetrable wall – denying me my desire to be who I felt I wanted to be. There was always a blockade, always a Mother or some other repressor, keeping me from metamorphosing into my true self. Suddenly I sensed that wall collapsing, these unknown yet familiar words rushing back to me as though I had long had an association with them. At that moment I really wanted to be a part of what these hooded beings said I was a part of. I was the last of something, I was important and I was necessary to whatever. It didn't matter what – it simply mattered that I *was*.

'We will show you yourself, who you really are. But, it will take time.'

'What next, then?'

'You must join us in our rituals, expand your mind alongside ours. We will assist in your re-connection with The Space.'

I did not question their apparent kindness, though I knew right off that they needed me. My power over them was absolute, but I didn't feel the need to exercise it at present. There was always time for that. There was time for all kinds of things. I could at any time pull out, put a stop to them and their schemes. But, I don't think I wanted to. I wanted to gain access to this mysterious thing they called The Space that I felt I did and didn't know at the same time.

The rest of my first visit was spent in a haze as I came to terms with what they were telling me. Much of it did not sink in, my recall of the finer details rather misty looking back now. I was but a teen, nearing adulthood but not quite there, and my mind was spread thin and wide. Something did stick in my mind, something which perhaps went some way to showing how loud my inner thoughts were to their ears – they told me to listen to their thoughts before I left for the day.

'It is not wise to involve yourself with Lucy Davies,' they warned me from nowhere. I was just standing there, trying to absorb more and more intricate notions.

'Why not?' I questioned in my naivety.

'You are destined to be with somebody else.'

'Who?' I was intrigued. This teenage virgin, keen to get his first leg over, was loathe to be kept waiting any longer. The sniff of a girl out there with my name on her was a veritable opportunity. But, they would not reveal who.

'It is not yet time,' is all they would say. I was not going to heed their advice. All they had done was set my mind to utter determination where the acquisition of Lucy was concerned. This other girl, who was she? Did she even exist, or was it one of their tricks? People had always tricked me, played games on me, made me the butt of their jokes. Lucy looked to me now like something I desperately wanted to get above all else. My only redemption in this utter objectivity was that I strove long and hard that night, alone in my bed, to picture Lucy the person and not just the body. Yes, she had been rather distant from me at school and we had had no real connection in life yet, but I could just feel deep down that she was the girl for me. And I would acquire her.

That morning, at breakfast, Father had already left early for work. He was almost a non-event in my life, our interactions with each other long since vanquished for no particular reason. We had once engaged on some mediocre level – constructing models together and the like – but I was growing up and he was not the sort of man to move along with me. We never spoke about anything fundamental, about anything less basic than the weather; he was unable to even introduce me to "the birds and the bees". I was left alone to develop and fix my own impression of "getting the girl", and now I felt such a point nearing. Stuart sat across from me, grinning just a little too much. I don't know what he had to grin about. Was the prospect of a day of school ahead of him cause for such mirth? Being that little bit younger than me, he still had a yard's length to go before finishing his educational stint, but somehow I felt less advanced than he. That grin was all it took to make me feel he knew something I didn't, or had done something I hadn't. It took me all my strength not to yell at him and cause a scene. But, I wouldn't let him have that.

'What are you plans for the day, Peter?' he suddenly asked me in a sly tone.

'Yes, Peter, what *are* your plans for the day?' Mother rounded, squaring her eyes at mine as she joined us at the table with a slice of toast slathered in marmalade.

'I have important work to undertake down at the police station,' said I, deciding to at least attempt some sort of fabrication.

'What important work?' Stuart carried on, that nasty glint in his eye as the morning sun caught his bright blonde hair. I ducked away, surprised by its intensity.

'Speak up,' Mother roared. 'Another day of fannying around, is it?' She took in a mouthful of toast, and carried on talking: 'You need a job, Peter, not this obsession with solving local mysteries.'

'But, I feel drawn to it, Mother,' I cut in gingerly, shielding my face from the onslaught of moist toast shards shooting from her open mouth. Stuart giggled. 'I feel the need to solve crimes.'

'Rubbish! You're wasting your life, Peter. You need a job, not a passion. You don't want to end up one of these middle-aged losers living on welfare at home with their mothers, do you?'

I felt rather broken by this. Still, it was nothing new. I'd heard the same thing day in day out since finishing school, and Stuart knew exactly how to initiate such diatribes. That was how we left the discussion, for soon enough I had finished my own breakfast and headed out on my bicycle to Myrtleville police station. There, I knew I would find, amongst other interesting things, Lucy Davies. Short, dark-haired and round-bottomed, she was a sight almost too overbearing to look at. If you stared for too long, it would result in the extermination of your sight – nothing more would you wish to look upon, as you'd have already seen it all. We had very much hated each other at school, but now that the bonds and restraints of such a tired institutional set-up were banished from our young lives, we could go about constructing some form of connection.

She passed me in the main reception as I entered the station. I went to say hello, but she was already gone – possibly from my day altogether. Would there be another opportunity to see her again today? This drew the air from my lungs, the strength from my legs. I thought about going after her, then decided against it. I sat down and mulled things over. Then, she walked past again, heading back the way she'd come. I stood up and stepped towards her.

'Lucy,' I greeted her, 'hi!'

'Hi,' she said back, carrying on her way. She pushed the double doors ahead of her open and stepped through. I followed beside her, covertly drawing in her scent when proximity permitted. 'What do you want?' she asked, stopping and turning to face me.

'Good question,' was all I could respond with. She rolled her eyes and carried on. 'Actually, I, erm,' I thought, her pace difficult to allow thinking time. 'I was wondering if you wanted to, you know…'

'No, I don't know,' she responded indifferently, reaching Inspector Hastings' door.

'Go out with me.' I took the plunge, empowered by the ego

boost dealt to me by the museum club. All she did was laugh in my face, before knocking on the door.

'Come in,' Hastings called out, and she did so, closing the door in my face.

For me, that went better than I could have ever expected. She could easily have spat in my face, or head-butted me, for instance. That I was still standing, and not floored by her might, was proof that things could soon begin to blossom between us. I turned to look down the corridor to see Sergeant Noose walking towards me. With him was a rather attractive woman dressed in a suit similar to his own. She had her hair permed, making her look older than she was, and the shoulder pads did not help either. Noose had her in hysterics as he blasted out some anecdote. They reached me and his spirits soured.

'What do you want, Peter?' he asked me, clearly wanting to carry on his wooing.

'Aren't you going to introduce me to your lady friend?' I asked coyly.

'She is not my lady friend, Peter, she is Detective Sergeant Nicola Williams, and she's here to speak to Lucy Davies about career options.'

'Ah, I see. Maybe you could speak to me too,' I hinted, wishing to join the force myself. I saw it as a veritable chance to kill two birds with one stone. Mother wanted me to have a job, and I wanted to solve mysteries. It made perfect sense to become a copper.

Noose laughed at me, knocking on Hastings' door.

'Come in,' Hastings called out, and Noose and Williams did so, slamming the door in my face.

I made my way back to reception and sat there in a stupor for the next hour or so. Noose and Williams eventually passed me and headed out, either not seeing me at all or possibly ignoring me on purpose. Then, Lucy came through the double doors. She caught sight of me and initially carried on past. But, something made her stop in her tracks and turn. She came over and I stood as she reached me.

'I'm sorry about earlier, Peter. I was nervous about my interview,' she said. My heart stopped beating for but a split second and I wished I'd still been sitting.

'No worries,' was all I could say.

'It's not that, well, it's not that I don't like you or anything, but I don't want to get distracted in my studies.'

'Yes, of course.'

She smiled. Oh, she was such a beauty. 'It's funny really, you asking me out.'

'It is?'

'Well, it probably sounds a little odd to say this, but I kinda had a little crush on you when we were little kids in school.' She chuckled. 'Seems really funny looking back now. I used to imagine us playing house together, but your mother would never let you come round to play when my mother asked.'

The fury of a millennia of human suffering flushed through my fists right that second. 'That is quite funny,' I lied. 'And I thought you hated me.'

'Well I didn't like you later on, when I started to fancy boys properly.' Again she laughed. This was the first proper conversation we'd ever had. Why had I been so foolish as to just ask her out on the spot with no prior connection to back it up? This was that connection I was striving for, being created right now.

'I didn't like you, either,' I giggled childishly, smiling. She smiled back, getting the joke. 'Listen, sorry for asking you out earlier. I was nervous too, just being stupid I was.'

'No, no!'

'So, how did your interview go?'

'Very well, thanks,' she responded very positively indeed, a jump in her gait.

'Well I'm here if you need any assistance! I know lots about the place, I'm quite keen on fighting crime,' I said.

'Thanks, I'll remember that.'

As she walked away I felt her drawing closer to me than ever before.

* * *

A few months had passed now, and my "visits" to the museum club had continued apace. They had not mentioned Lucy since that very first meeting, and nor had I. But, she was at the forefront of my mind at all times. She had since moved out of her parents house into a flat near the police station. I had offered my help in her moving in, and been honoured with the task of some heavy lifting. She had rewarded me with a coffee on a couple of occasions, and we had shared hours of notes about various murder cases in the local area over the years. She seemed to relish reading up about the most brutal of crimes, never fazed by the ever heinous nature of them.

One tuesday evening, whilst playing whist with Mother and Aunt Sally down at the local community centre, I won a cheap bottle of wine on the raffle. I kept it for a week or more, wondering what to do with it. Stuart was keen that he sample some, but I declined his request.

'Lucy and I are going to have it,' I told him.

'Lucy,' he laughed. 'You'll never get in her knickers.'

'You're so base, so tiresome,' I shot back.

'And you're not even anywhere near her level, dickwad,' he laughed again. 'She wouldn't shag you if you were the last man on earth. She's just stringing you along like a little donkey, getting you to run errands for her.'

'Fuck you,' I spat, sick of his poison.

'I've got more of a chance with her,' was his deluded continuance of this pile of tosh. 'I'm more her type.'

'And what's that, a tosser?'

'Let's face it, Pete, I've got the looks… and the brains, for that matter.'

I left him to his little thoughts, resolving to prove him wrong. I felt my superiority over him, and many others, growing with each new meeting I had with the museum club. They understood me, to an extent, and even though it did feel peculiar and almost like some form of theistic ritual, I continued to attend their gatherings. I was welcomed and encouraged in the widening of my thoughts. Yes, I kept quiet about Lucy due to their apparent disapproval, but everything else about it was fine. Never did I see their faces, but I heard their voices and repeated and learnt the words they spoke. There was much to hear about my apparent past lives, and how I had been one of the first to connect with The Space hundreds of years ago. It sounded at once fanciful, but equally as believable. I wanted to believe, I wanted it to be true. Eventually, as the months wore on, I could almost hear The Space talking to me. I had a strange vision, snippets of past lives playing out in my mind. One even showed the future, where my current body was aged and I had a daughter named Chloe. I appeared to be a single parent, and this troubled me somewhat. Was Lucy the mother, or somebody else? And, what had happened to her? One day they thought I was "ready" for "stage two" of the process I appeared to be going through, and they presented me with a train ticket for a journey I was to undertake the very next day. I would travel across town to a cemetery where I would truly feel The Space running through me.

That evening I rang the bell to Lucy's flat, and she let me in. I had the wine, and offered it to her. Reluctantly she took it, suggesting we open it there and then and consume it together. We had a recently solved case to toast, and I was not going to say no to drinking in her company. Soon the bottle was gone and I was wishing we had another. Suddenly Lucy presented one, and we began at that one too.

'We've become close friends lately, Lucy,' I started, both of us still sitting at her tiny kitchen table. Her flat was little more than one room, but I guess it *was* a haven away from any parents or siblings.

'We have, you're right! Who'd have thought it, we hated each other in school!' she laughed.

'I never hated you, Lucy,' I drunkenly gushed. 'I just thought you too gorgeous to ever fancy any one like me back. I had no confidence.'

'And have you any confidence now?'

'Confidence for what?' I asked naively.

'To lean in and try to kiss me.'

'Oh, I see. Hmm, I dunno. Will you slap me?'

'Why don't you find out?'

I did lean in, and she slapped me lightly and playfully, pulling my head closer so we could embrace. It was everything I had expected it to be and more – my first ever kiss with the ultimate girl. I was in heaven, our lips and tongues uniting and jousting as if they'd been doing it for centuries. We were both, perhaps, a little new to this, and neither quite knew how to proceed. It did not, therefore, immediately lead to the bedroom, but what did occur in the kitchen was beyond anything I had thus far experienced in life.

I awoke the next morning, half naked, next to her on the sofa. My mind was hazy, my head pounding. She was still sleeping, but soon stirred to find me sitting up and staring down at her.

'Hey,' she said.

'Hey,' I replied, unsure how she might react. Was it all a drunken mistake last night, or truly the culmination of our undeniable bond? She rubbed her eyes before stretching her arms. 'I enjoyed last night.'

'Me too.' We sat in silence for a moment, before I cleared my throat. 'Lucy, I think I love you.' I think I did.

'You're good at just blurting these things out, aren't you?!'

'Sorry, it's too soon. I just, I just don't want you to think I'm some user or a snake or anything.'

She took my hand. 'I love you too, Peter,' she said rather casually through a yawn, 'you're really sweet.' She placed her hand on my chest and rested her head on it. 'We've got something really nice going here. Let's get married!' she giggled. 'That'll cause a stir.'

'*Will* you marry me?' I asked her, deadly serious.

'Of course!'

I don't know how serious she was, but I was. This was the most successful thing that I could perhaps ever hope for in life, aside from The Space. No, this could be even more successful than that. This was truly real, and right here right now. I could really stick it to Stuart with this one. She caught sight of the time, and I sensed she wanted to get on doing something. She was not for lazing around. Besides, I did have my "big day" with the museum club ahead. That seemed somewhat immaterial and small now compared to what had happened between Lucy and me.

'I'm not due in to the station until this afternoon, but I have a mountain of studying. I must get on,' she said.

I knew how important it was to her, and was not about to stand in her way. That could come later, when we had truly established something more solid. I got washed and left her. It still wasn't half eight and I suddenly thought about Stuart again. He was on his final exam study break from school, his step into adulthood coming as fast as mine appeared to be. He'd probably still be in bed, but I couldn't wait to brag. I called home from the phone box outside Lucy's flat to goad him with my news. Mother answered, and she was both furious and relieved to hear my voice.

'Where are you, what have you been doing?' she cried at me. But, all I wanted to do was tell Stuart. Eventually she put him on and his reaction was not what I had expected. He was rather congratulatory.

* * *

I made for the railway station on foot, embarking on my journey across town to the cemetery I'd been instructed to go to. When I arrived, there was a funeral in progress. I held back, watching from afar as a coffin was lowered into its final resting place. Soon the mourners dispersed and I made my way to the fresh grave as two middle-aged men in overalls began shovelling in soil. They didn't speak to me and I didn't speak to them, and there was no gravestone to mark the plot's occupant.

Looking around, I caught sight of one of the hooded figures standing over a grave in the distance. I had never seen any of them alone before. They had always been united as six, never split or separate. I headed over, coming to stand by their side. I looked at the gravestone. It was old and tired, lichen-ridden and hardly legible. I crouched down, squinting. It read "RIP Peter Smith 1859-1895".

'Same name as me,' I noted to the hooded figure.

'It *is* you. You have lived many lives throughout history.'

'Am I always called Peter Smith?'

'Labels are unimportant. It could so easily read a myriad of other names you have gone under.'

'Then why doesn't it?'

'You are Peter Smith now, so you see your other selves as Peter Smith also.'

I studied the gravestone again. 'Thirty-six. I wasn't very old, was I?'

'It is a difficult age to live past, being as it was your original self's set of years.'

Was I destined to forever re-live an existence of thirty-six years, going on until time itself ceased to be? I could not tell, and didn't want to ask. For some reason it already felt like I had lived my current life numerous times before, trapped in this body and unable to move forward to my next life in the future. What was holding me back?

'Where are the others?' I asked.

'Waiting.'

'Waiting where, and for what?'

'Stretch your mind to The Space, seek out the answers yourself.'

I looked long and hard at the gravestone. Perhaps the museum club had thought coming here and presenting me with a prior self would re-jig my memory. There was only the slight inkling of something other than imagination in my mind – I could see somebody dead, somebody sprawled on the floor covered in blood. The vision wouldn't allow me specifics, nor even a hint at a clue. All I knew was that this person had been murdered. I turned to look again at the figure, but I was now alone. There was nothing left for me to do but return home. But first, I wanted to see Lucy again. She would probably not be at her flat, no doubt having gone to the police station by now. Still, I didn't want to see her there. I wanted to see her at the flat. That was where we could continue our bodily embrace. I decided to go there and wait for her return, whereby we could carry on where we had left off early this morning. Entrusted with a spare key over a month before that I'd never used up until now, I was able to let myself in. I knew she wouldn't mind, not now we were engaged.

I walked into the hallway. It was dark, the curtains still drawn. I opened them and walked into the living room. Words cannot describe the sight that awaited me. There was Lucy, crawled on the carpet and covered in blood. She was naked, her battered body left in a heap like a discarded pile of rubble.

I dropped to my knees, weeping, shaking her and begging her to wake up.

* * *

The police had me lined up as her killer, and this was too much to contend with. I became cold, uncooperative and disruptive to their neat plans for a tidy case. Noose was the only one who believed me, for no other reason than he just did; but he had his own problems. As he was leading me through the police reception one day during investigations, his wife and their young son charged in and began yelling abuse at him.

'How could you do this to your family?' she was screeching, the tears flowing and her face bright red. She was certainly older than her husband, and looked rather drawn and lifeless with it too. There was something not altogether sincere about her tears. Indeed, why had she come to Noose's place of work to have this argument? 'Where is she then?' she went on.

'Go away Sam, I'm working.'

'Look,' she carried on, yanking at her son's arm and pushing him at Noose. 'Just look at what you're ruining for a quick fling with that slut Nicola.' The boy looked up at his father, puzzled and as angry as his mother.

'Please, we'll have this discussion later. I must get on with Peter's case.'

'Ah, so this is *the* Peter Smith you're so obsessed with, is it? Don't bother coming home, Henry, we're finished.' She stormed off, dragging the boy with her.

'But, Sam, wait,' he called back.

She turned back in the doorway, shouting: 'Always about the job with you, never about your family. Well, you enjoy yourself. Poor Gary doesn't even know who his father is these days. He never sees you now, and he never will again.' She left, the door swinging open and shut for nearly a minute afterwards due to her force.

'Bit awkward, that,' I said to Noose, trying to look sympathetic. I was not really in the mood for sympathy – nobody had shown me any – but this sergeant had at least shown me some form of care and interest. I tried desperately to block all the hurt and torment from my mind. Lucy was everything to me, I just had to make her nothing or her senseless and barbaric murder would be my undoing.

* * *

Following my acquittal for Lucy's murder I should have been in utter turmoil at her death, but I had done well to block the emotions. My only thoughts were a wish that I had actually been the one who murdered her, then at least I'd have known who did it. Not knowing was almost as painful as the loss of her, which I had come to terms with in my compartmental way. She was a section in my life, and each section had its place. There was an order, and I'd be damned if I was not going to maintain that order. One such order was my membership of the museum club, which they had told me was for life. I returned, the first time in over a year since Lucy's death, little knowing I was stepping into yet another bout of madness.

The room where they gathered, and where I had first met them, was simply no longer there. The door had been removed from its hinges, opening the space that once lay behind it out and now part of the corridor outside. There were no barriers, no sheaths to conceal its contents. The walls had been whitewashed and a few paintings by local artists hung lazily upon them. I walked around studying them for a while, not quite knowing what to do. One painting caught my eye. It was of a light blue flat cap sitting on a wooden stool in the middle of a bare room, and it was just credited to "Anonymous". It seemed to have no meaning whatsoever, serving no purpose at all for the viewer. Then, I turned and saw that very same light blue flat cap sitting on a wooden stool in the middle of the room. I felt sure it hadn't been there when I first came in. Still, nothing surprised or shocked me anymore. A simple hat on a simple stool was simply nothing to me. I'm not saying it wasn't a nice hat, because it was. Presently I stepped up to the stool and picked the hat up. It was ice cold, almost painfully so, but soft also. So soft was it, that I was dying to try it on. If only it hadn't been so cold. I wanted it to be nice and warm and then it began to change temperature. Rather quickly, in fact, until it was just the way I wanted it to be. I put it on and it fit perfectly. Turning back to the painting, it was now a mirror and I studied my reflection. The hat aged me, perhaps, but I liked it. Finders, keepers. I strolled back out of the room with my new hat and bumped into a little old lady halfway down the corridor.

'Tell me, young man,' she said to me, 'can you tell me where the hat exhibition is?'

'I cannot, I'm afraid,' I replied, looking around for a directional clue. The old one looked up and squinted at my face.

'Do I know you? You look familiar.'

Quickly I moved along, not wanting her to associate me with any recent events that had occurred. I was not that person, I was not a part of that.

I kept on going, one corridor leading to another, and yet another. Endless, identical lines of space bringing my person deeper and deeper into the warren of the museum. Eventually I hit a dead end, a sign on the wall in front of me reading "NO WAY OUT. TURN BACK". I tried to turn back, but felt the uncontrollable urge to push on in spite of the impersonal command. I heard voices behind me, the museum club members no longer talking in unison but trying to block each other out.

'Reaping Icon is within these three,' one called out. I turned to face them. Three were kneeling down, their heads bowed. The other three were standing behind them, each one holding a knife to the one kneeling below them.

'Reaping Icon is within us all,' one of the kneeling cried out.

'We must sacrifice you for the good of preserving the final link.' With this, the knives were dragged across the throats of the three kneeling figures and they collapsed in pools of their own blood. I was stunned into silence, again believing I was probably just watching a horror film on TV as the three slayers proceeded to mutilate the faces of the deceased. Stricken with a detached complacency that I would somehow not be harmed, I lost myself in thoughts of my new hat and could not bring myself to catch a glimpse of any of the faces of the figures – be they alive, or dead. If I did not believe it had just happened, then it could not have just happened. Who did my hat belong to originally? Why had they just left it on the stool? Maybe they'd left it behind by accident and would be looking for it right now. Had I done the right thing by just helping myself to it? Maybe not, but to blazes with them! It was my hat now, and I was damned if I was going to relinquish ownership of it.

To ever think upon that not requested,
The juvenile expression of wanton regret -
If ever there impressed a mind its own,
Would deviation be a gladness?

Poppycock, gobbledygook,
And all that jazz –
Open to nothing but nothing;
A life for a life.

WHAT HAPPENED
TO NOOSE NEXT
(PART TWO)

Peter looked over at the three hooded figures and grimaced. 'You're murderers, and you got away with it.'

'Ending the lives of the other three was a necessity to try and halt the spread of Reaping Icon – he had destroyed their minds.'

'Had he?!'

Noose coughed, the damp of the hole affecting his chest. He, beginning to accept Peter's return to life, turned to face the hooded figures also. 'I remember those three murders in the museum. It was like a sacrifice, the bodies all defaced and dismembered. You're fucking evil.' He scratched his chin. 'Is that what I'm here for, to be sacrificed?'

'No, you are here to assist Peter Smith.'

'Was Reaping Icon in Lucy?' Peter growled. 'Is that why you murdered her?'

'We did not murder Lucy. We did warn you, however. We tried to stop the inevitable from happening.'

'What do you mean by that? What inevitable?'

'Long ago, a prior life of yours was shown a vision by The Space purporting to the murder of Lucy. Can you not remember? We wanted to stop it.'

'Then why didn't you just tell me that?' Peter cried out, grabbing hold of one of them and pulling them close. 'She could have lived, you idiots.'

'We have failed in stopping the spread of Reaping Icon, but in bringing you back there is hope,' was their reply. Peter twisted the figure he had a hold of around and yanked the hood off. With the head exposed, they turned around to face Peter. It *was* Peter, looking directly at himself. He stepped back from them as the other two removed their hoods to reveal two more Peter's. 'Our time is complete, we must collectively die.' They each brought out a knife and placed it against their necks. 'Only one Peter Smith can succeed. Let us end this sick curse.' They dragged the knives across their own throats with a severe force, blood gushing forth as they writhed around in pain and confusion. Noose tried his best to try and stop the blood flowing from one of them, ripping his shirt in half and wrapping it around the wound. It was no good, nobody could help them now. Peter felt empty, like he'd been abandoned in infancy by a troubled single parent. Noose kept valiantly on, soaked in blood and weeping in frustration. Eventually he collapsed in a heap on the floor, pulling his thin sweaty hair off his face and covering his head in blood in the process.

'How are they you? They were all you!'

'It's a mystery,' was Peter's quick reply.

'So what happens now?' Noose sighed, looking up at Peter.

'We clear your name, and we finally bring Lucy's murderer to justice too.'

Noose stayed in his heap, exhausted. 'Beth and Dani Henderson were the next-door neighbours of Anna, Lucy's mum,' he whispered, not quite wanting to go down that road with Peter. It had always been a thorny subject, and he wasn't yet sure that Peter *was* ready to accept what happened to Lucy. He'd always been so good at blocking it from his mind and not only denying any part in her life, but also denying her existence altogether. Still, this Peter before him now did seem somewhat more stable than ever before. If that was at all possible. It was rather ironic that a man who'd committed suicide over ten years ago, and had somehow been delivered back to existence, could be stable. But there it was, and here Peter was. Noose struggled to his feet. Peter hadn't replied. He hadn't even flinched. 'How do we get out of here?' Noose asked him, as if Peter held all the answers to life's questions.

'I don't know.'

They looked around; there was no door, no entrance of any kind. The only thing apart from the walls was the slab Noose had been lying on. Peter turned to it and pulled at it. It opened on a hinge, revealing a set of steps leading into the darkness below. The two men struggled down them, feeling their way along horrid damp clay walls as they got deeper and deeper. Suddenly the steps stopped and the floor was flat, an inch of putrid still water lying on it. They walked down it, fighting the smell and the squelching, and reached a ladder stretching up into a narrow dark tube.

'Turns your stomach, this place,' Noose commented, trying to picture in his mind how the figures had managed to bring his unconscious body down here.

'I guess this is the exit,' was Peter's response as he ascended the ladder, very quickly reaching the top and finding a circular lid above his head. He slowly pushed it open, peeping out through it. It was a grid in the museum garden, and everywhere was dark. Lifting the grid and sliding it off, he got out and helped pull Noose out.

'So what was it like being dead?' Noose suddenly asked Peter.

'For me, it's been as frustrating as being alive.' Peter grinned in his old way, and Noose's spirits were lifted immeasurably. He grinned back.

'I guess I'll be a very wanted man, we won't be safe.'

'Indeed not.' Peter took in a deep breath of the fresh nighttime air. He caught the sweet scent of the abundant museum moonflowers and for a brief moment thought how wonderful life could be. 'We need to find somewhere to hide out and get tidied up.'

* * *

Lauren stumbled towards her flat door in her dressing gown, still half asleep and angry she'd been disturbed during some much-needed sleep. Deep down she knew she probably shouldn't even open it, or should at the very least call out and ask who it was, but maybe she sensed who it would be. Noose had escaped from the hospital and it was all over the news. She'd been offered a police guard in case he tried to contact her, but she'd refused. Nevertheless, there was a guard downstairs sitting in his car across from the entrance to the flats. He hadn't given it much thought when two women had approached the building, especially when they knew the code for the door and had gained access. They'd probably just been out on a late night bender, and were finding their way home at this rather late hour.

When Lauren opened the door she found these two women standing outside in the corridor. Well, not quite women, but the dark towels wrapped around their heads and the frilly frocks could have made them look a bit like women from a distance… in dim light.

'Why on Earth are you dressed like that?' was all Lauren could say. She was too gobsmacked, but not scared, at the sight of Peter and Noose. The latter she had helped build the forensic case against which sent him down for two counts of rape and murder, and the former she hadn't seen for over a decade. 'And how did you get into the block?'

'You are even more stunning than when last we met,' was Peter's response. He looked upon her thin frame and strained face, lines beginning to form here and there and her skin that much paler. She was still perfect to him; she always had been.

He looked for the birthmark on her neck, and felt he was coming home to where he belonged. But again, Lucy took hold of his mind and shook him. Where truly did he belong? Lucy was dead and Lauren was alive and in front of him. He could remember Lucy now, and with Lauren it was different. With Lauren it seemed to go beyond teenage lust and a coming-of-age search for sexuality. This was pain on top of pain where Lucy was concerned, because although he'd imagined them to be married at the time, he somehow felt it would never have worked out. Deep down he knew it was "young love" and a teenage fling. This made Lucy's life all the more wasted. She had never found that true one in which to spend it with, unlike Peter who now wanted to share his life with Lauren. One life, right here and now, to live out just once with her and never to return again. He wanted to grow old with her and die, and then call it a day.

'Where have you been all these years, why did you just ditch me from your life?' she shot back.

'It's complicated.'

'I bet it is.'

'Trust me Lauren,' Noose cut in, laughing nervously. 'It really is.'

She looked at Noose, some of the blood still on his face and hands. Lauren didn't know whether to laugh at the sight of them in dresses or scream for help from the guard downstairs. No, some gut feeling told her she would not be harmed by the pair. 'You're a wanted man.'

'I didn't kill them,' he yet again had to cry out, almost ready to just give up and admit to the murders. It seemed that everyone already thought he'd done it, so why continue to waste his energy fighting them? 'Look, just let us in. We have no one else to turn to.'

Lauren stepped aside, and they went in. 'You're not the only one on the run. That Alex who assassinated the PM just strolled out of prison. The guards let him go, apparently.'

'What?' Peter asked her, filled with dread.

'Yeah, he's got a lot of support. People are saying he was set up.'

'Reaping Icon,' Peter uttered.

'Who?' Lauren asked.

'Things are bad,' he replied, trying to take hold of Lauren's hand. She snatched it away. 'We've wasted enough time. I thought I'd never get the chance to see you again.'

'You could have come to see me any time you liked in the past ten years.'

'No. Really, I couldn't have.'

'Anyway, how *did* you get in? Security is tight around here at the moment,' Lauren carried on, turning her back and moving quickly across the room to the window. She edged the curtain open a crack and peeped down.

'I knew the code to the door,' Peter said. 'I can pull up a lot of information like that in my mind now.'

'And we nicked the clothes off a washing line,' Noose added.

'Never leave clothes out overnight!' Peter tried to joke. Lauren was not in the mood. She started trembling.

'Lauren, are you okay?' Noose asked her, though purposely kept back.

'Of course I'm not bloody okay. How am I supposed to be okay when you two just waltz back into my life?' Her tear ducts were bone dry, and she paced the room. Peter had a good look around – things hadn't changed since last time he was here. He remembered it well.

'We kissed last time I was in your flat,' he said to her, pulling up the memory in his mind. He too, though, now held back from her. Their presence was just beginning to sink in. She rubbed at her forehead, flicking the air randomly as she fought these old emotions. 'We had such plans.'

'Did we?' she mumbled. 'Did we?'

Noose coughed to get Peter's attention, shaking his head to try and deter him from pushing Lauren too much too soon.

'Look, Lauren,' Noose cut in, 'can we stay here just tonight and get cleaned up? I know it's a lot to ask.'

'Inspector Noose,' she started, turning to look at him. 'Whatever happened to you?'

'I wish I knew,' he sighed.

'You were so well-loved in the community.'

'I was? I thought I was a joke.'

'You were the best inspector that Myrtleville ever had. Now look at you, a convicted pedophile, rapist and murderer. No motive, just pure sexual depravity.'

'You know I didn't do it,' Noose whimpered, about ready to give in and just go along with what people said about him. He looked for the sofa and slumped onto it, not caring if the dress rode up and showed his hairy legs.

'The forensic case against you was watertight,' Lauren pointed out, her gaze keeping away from Peter. He just kept looking right at her, no longer in the mood to deny his desires. 'Somebody must really hate you.'

'Why would somebody harm those poor girls just to get at me?' Noose questioned, even he finding it difficult to believe. 'They never even discovered the identity of the woman I slept with.' He rubbed his eyes. 'Oh for fuck sake, I've just had enough. I really have had enough of everything.' His hands came away from his eyes and he found himself looking at Lauren's carpet. There, amongst the rather worn grey-green flower pattern, was the face. It was looking right at him, smiling. He looked up to the heavens, his fist clenching momentarily. 'I'm so tired of pleading my case. I just wish I was dead.' Peter, reluctance not even a brief thought, came to sit next to him and put his arm around him. Lauren couldn't help thinking it an amusing sight, the pair of them sitting there hugging in frilly frocks; a smile twitched on her lips and she made the concerted effort to push any further emotion down into the pit of her stomach. There it gurgled and bubbled away, a fierce pain striking her. She mustn't let it show, she thought – she couldn't let this invasion into her focused life cause any upset. 'I've been so lonely,' Noose sobbed like a little child, grasping hold of Peter's face and drawing it close. He rubbed his friend's cheek and drew it close, pressing his against it. Tears came to Peter's eyes too, and the men clasped each other tight for what seemed to Lauren like an age. Their chests jerked in and out as they let it all out, neither wanting to let go for fear of the other leaving. Noose was the child, comforted by this ceaseless liver of humankind who had returned to him.

'You turned your back on me, Noose,' Peter cried, turning the tables to allow Noose the adulthood. 'Last time I saw you, in the hospital, you walked out and left me.'

'It doesn't matter now, Peter. None of it matters,' Noose told him. Now Peter was the child, Noose comforting and reassuring him.

Lauren was completely at a loss as to what to do. Part of her wanted to drop her wall and collapse into the two men and feel their comfort right now, and yet the mindset kept pushing through to keep her distanced from them. She had kept herself at a distance from everyone these past few years. When she had dropped her guard and let someone in, it had ended in utter tragedy. She wasn't prepared to put herself through that wreck again. Her body wouldn't allow it anyway – its own innate failsafe protected her from even feeling the touch of another being. The dead could not touch her, and this was what made her job as part of the forensics team so perfect. She was utterly at home poking and prodding all those corpses. When it came to the living, hurting, mess that was now on her sofa… Well, she just physically couldn't go to them. To touch the living – to allow herself to embrace and indeed be embraced – was to open the flood defence and ultimately drown again. Too long had she forced herself down this path. She couldn't envisage coming back.

Time passed, and Noose had fallen asleep in Peter's arms. He edged away, letting the exhausted man carry on his slumber. Lauren had settled onto a stool and seemed her usual distant self. She wasn't so much settled on the stool as fixed down, no longer pacing up and down. Peter got up off the sofa, not in need of rest like Noose, and stood still across from Lauren for a moment. He had been dead for a decade, though it could so easily have been just seconds. Time didn't exist in the waiting room. 'How have you been?' he whispered to Lauren. For a time she didn't respond, staying fixed as if in a trance. To hear his voice again after so long was both pleasure and torment in equal amounts. The years had allowed all the unpleasantries to kind of fade, so that now all that really stood in her way was herself. She couldn't really remember specifics anymore. She'd played events over and over in her head at the time, but after a while she'd just started blocking them out. Eventually she looked up at Peter. Their eyes met, but she did not alter her stern countenance.

'I've been plodding on,' she replied.

'Life just passes sometimes, doesn't it.'

'Life!' she laughed, choking briefly on what could only be a battle of suppressing any outward signs of feeling. 'Life does just pass. It keeps on going no matter who or who isn't in it.' She looked over at Noose. 'It was a big blow, what happened to Henry. It upset what we all had going.'

'Are you happy, Lauren?' he outright asked her, still keeping his physical distance.

'Are you?' she turned it back, forcing a grin.

'I'd be happy if I could spend the rest of my life with you.'

A laugh jerked from her lips. 'Really? So you come back after all these years, just barge right back into my life and lay that out on the table? You've got a nerve.' He kept on looking at her, desperate for her to want him. 'Took you ten years to think that one up, did it?'

'Do you want to know the truth?'

'What truth?'

'I've been dead,' he admitted, having to smile at her because even he found it a bit silly to say. 'You won't believe me, but I've lived many times before, both in this present form and others in the past.'

'You've lost your mind.'

'Maybe I have.' He stepped towards her and her entire body shook, but she quickly regained her composure as he slowly sat down across from her at the table. 'I've spent the last ten years just waiting in nothingness, waiting to return to the life I was desperate to depart.'

'But, but,' she replied, shaking her head but somehow feeling she aught to accept what she was hearing. It did, after all, sound so familiar to her.

'I sank so low, so utterly terrible that I felt I couldn't go on. I ended my life, Lauren, knowing full well I could never actually die forever. Always I have to come back, trapped by a *gift* of never ending life.' He put his hand on the table. She looked down at it. 'I'm just a walking, talking corpse spouting a pile of unbelievable rubbish. I am dead.'

Lauren's hand came on the table and rested on top of his. She was trembling, and so cold. 'You're very warm for a corpse,' she said, feeling his moist hot hand. 'Believe me, I've touched a lot of corpses in my time.'

Peter brought his other hand out and clasped hers. 'I've made a lot of mistakes in my time, spread a lot of poison. All I want is to live out the rest of this current life with you. I don't want to come back again, I just want one fulfilling life.'

'And I can give you that? Really?'

'Yes, you can.'

'How?'

'By just being here for me when I get back.'

She pulled her hand away. 'Get back? You're not leaving me again?'

'I must stop Reaping Icon, and find Lucy's killer. Only then will I be able to cut The Space off forever.'

'And how will you manage all that?' she asked him, almost wanting to think she was just humouring him, but deep down completely buying into it all.

'I have opened my mind back to The Space, I am whole again. Its power will allow me to achieve some things.'

'Like wooing me?' she asked angrily, getting up and pacing again.

'I would never trick you into anything. I couldn't live with myself if I did that.' He too stood up, walking over to the kitchen. 'If you don't want me after all is, then that's just something I'll have to live with.' He started opening her kitchen cupboards, eyeing up the contents within.

'What are you doing, what are you looking for?' she snapped, marching over to him and pushing his hand away from her precious units.

'I'm ever so thirsty.'

At first she glared at him, but soon a smile formed. It was a genuine smile, and Peter just knew that beyond all the crap that was going on she really did want to be with him. She walked over to the fridge and, opening it, brought out a carton of milk. Peter's eyes rolled into the back of his head as she tried to hide a little giggle.

* * *

The following morning Peter peeped out of the window to see Lauren getting into the unmarked police car. It drove off, leaving the coast clear for he and Noose to exit. Noose had cleaned himself up and, forced into a pair of Lauren's trousers like Peter, didn't look too bad. Luckily Lauren wasn't really the kind to sport overtly revealing skirts and tops, so some of her more generic clothing was quite suitable for them. He stepped out of the bathroom as Peter pulled away from the window and flicked his eyes over to the laptop on the kitchen table.

'What?' Noose asked him, not quite with it yet.

'Take a look.'

Noose went to the laptop, sitting down and reading with increasing perplexity what he found on the screen. 'Barbara Davies,' he mumbled.

'Yes, released from prison just before Beth and Dani Henderson were murdered, and the woman you shagged,' Peter explained rather joyously. Noose looked up from the screen, raising an eyebrow, to see Peter's face beaming with excitement.

'You think Barbara murdered them, to set me up?'

'It's a distinct possibility, isn't it?!'

'Is that what The Space is telling you?' Noose snarled somewhat, highly uneasy about the deaths and his role in them.

'I hear hints and whispers about it.'

'Seems to me the only thing The Space is good for is giving you the security code to Lauren's flat,' Noose sighed. His eyes went back to the screen, reading again the news article explaining Barbara's case all those years ago when she'd murdered Louis Sellers and James Harrington. Perhaps Peter was onto something. 'But why, and how?'

'Well as the investigating officer or whatever, *you* were responsible for putting her inside. Maybe she fancied some revenge,' Peter surmised.

Noose looked at him again and almost smiled. For the first time in a long while he had somebody on his case, somebody supporting him. Then again, Nicola Williams *had* given him the key to the handcuffs in hospital. He had to focus, starting to puzzle over the logistics of what Barbara would have had to do in order to frame him.

'She'd have had to get some of my sperm and put it in Dani and Beth.'

'Had you had sex around the time, before the decapitation girl?'

Noose looked a little sheepish. 'No.'

'Wanked?' Peter asked, feigning an air of studious indifference.

'Probably,' Noose reluctantly admitted. 'A man's needs.' He rubbed his eyes. 'I, er, I'd generally wank into a condom,' he went on professionally, affecting a rather softer voice.

'Would you now?'

'I used to get these ones with a special substance in the lubrication which delayed it, you know. That way I'd last longer.'

'What a night in for the modern, single middle-aged man,' Peter chuckled. Noose frowned. 'So, presumably you binned these instead of flushing as every good boy does?' Noose nodded. 'Barbara got hold of one or more of these out of your bin and, hey presto, your jizz gets inside those reluctant cadavers.' Peter now sighed, dropping his light air. 'That Barbara is a strong woman, I remember my encounter with her.'

'Built like a brick shit house.'

'Yes. I dread to think what horrors she inflicted on those poor women. And the child, so sickening.' He turned his back on Noose and went again to the window, lowering his voice. 'All just to frame you. She would have hired the one you did shag. Probably a prostitute.'

Before all this ever happened, Noose had made the egotistical mistake of contemplating such attention. For somebody to want to frame him, he thought, would mean his life and work meant something. Somebody cared enough about him to go to such lengths. Of course, when it had eventually happened, it was a great ego destroyer and not the boost he had misguidedly coveted. Such things were as they are, and he could not go back and change his prior mindset. Or, perhaps he could? He looked over at Peter, the once-dead man back to life and in his life like never before. The roles were switched; he was now the one on the run with Peter as his champion. Still, Peter probably owed him that much. Noose had helped him out of trouble more times than he could remember. This was payback – not that he wanted paying back. He'd much rather have the roles switched back again as they used to be. Perhaps that's what had drawn him to Peter in the first place, the fact he could always play the role of champion and save the downtrodden from the unthinking and bloodthirsty mass. His desire to help people, to bring justice to the similarly downtrodden, had spectacularly backfired in his face and led to the utter collapse of his entire life. And yet, the one who, for the last ten years, he'd felt he couldn't save in the end was back and helping to save him.

'So, what do we do now?' Noose mused.

'We force the truth out of her.'

'I don't know what I'll do,' Noose admitted, 'if I clap eyes on the one who framed me. Woman or not, I might not be able to control myself.'

'I will be there, Noose; I'll hold you back.'

'Will you?' He stood up, pouring some water into a glass and downing it. 'Do we even know where she's living, anyway?'

Peter smirked. 'Of course we do. I took the liberty of accessing the online police files with Lauren's password.'

'Never change, do you!'

* * *

They had made their way on foot, which was still quite a

struggle for Noose. However, he had certainly rallied around since Peter's return and they both now crouched behind a hedge at the end of a field. The other side of the hedge lay Barbara Davies' garden and house, and Noose's anger had been steadily building.

'I think I might kill her,' he said calmly, getting up. Peter pulled him back down.

'Steady, Noose. We don't know for sure it's her yet, do we? Besides, you don't want to actually end up being a murderer, do you?'

'She deserves to die after what she did.'

Peter couldn't very well disagree with that. He knew as soon as he came across Lucy's killer that he'd likely kill them. No, he would definitely kill them. It was justice. But for now, they were sorting justice out for Dani and Beth Henderson and the decapitated woman. Their killer did deserve to die for what they did.

The hedge was rather high – too high to jump over, and besides, that would draw too much attention – and it stretched at the back of dozens of houses. The two men lay flat on their stomachs and looked under it. It would be a squeeze, beset with thorns and rotting litter, but it was the only way to go. There was no turning back. What would greet them when they reached the house? Would Barbara even be in? They struggled under and kept flat as they just made it through. Unperturbed by the thorn scratches to their backs, the pair kept flat on the ground and pulled themselves along in the thick grass until they met the back of a shed. Sitting up against it, they took a breather.

'So, a, er,' Noose fumbled, wondering how best to approach the subject. Peter gave out a little yawn, which Noose caught. 'I'm the only one who can remember you being dead?' he asked through his own yawn.

'Yup, pretty much,' was Peter's casual reply. He looked at Noose, grinning.

'It's mad, it's crazy.'

'It was necessary I'm afraid.' He looked away at the hedge, twiddling his thumbs. 'Without you present, the museum club may not have been able to bring me back.'

'Why?'

'Well,' Peter responded sheepishly, 'you are my strongest tie to the here and now, you were the one my entity could latch onto.'

'So I was like a host?'

'Yes, I was like a wasp laying my eggs in your fruity goodness,' Peter laughed.

'What about Lauren? You told her you loved her, shouldn't she be your strongest tie or whatever?'

'Things aren't as simple as that,' Peter shot.

'They never are, are they?' Noose sighed. 'Those men, the museum men… They were all *you*.'

Peter, not uneasy about Noose's ponderances, nonetheless wanted to get this latest problem wrapped up, so poked his head around the shed to clock the various windows in both Barbara's house and the houses either side. There were plenty that could potentially accommodate a spoiler of their plans. Either way, the chance had to be taken. He mouthed '3-2-1' to Noose before stepping out from behind the shed and scurrying on all fours towards the house. Noose followed, keeping up with him on pure adrenalin. Soon they had reached the house and, backs against the wall, took a breather.

'It's rather unfortunate, really,' Peter whispered.

'What is?'

'All this, everything that's happened and is happening to you. You don't deserve it.'

'Don't I? Are you sure about that?'

Peter knew he most certainly did not, but Noose himself wasn't so sure. Something he'd done to somebody in the past must have brought this on. If indeed Barbara Davies was the one who'd done this, then it was his fault for putting her in prison for a decade. She'd originally killed because of the one she'd loved. Was that a definite crime?

Peter slid sideways along the wall and reached the back door, trying the handle. It was unlocked. Easing it open ever so slightly, he stuck his nose into the gap and sniffed the released air from within the house. Something didn't smell altogether pleasant, though he wasn't a master of smells. In fact, now he took the time to question why he'd even smelt the air in the first place. It was an animal instinct, not something he should be doing. Then again, he *was* an animal. At present, at least. Reluctantly he reached for that section in his mind where he had tried to force his connection to The Space, trying as he'd done when working out the key code to Lauren's flat to harness some residual energy to aid him in his quest. Silence. He looked back at Noose, who was nodding encouragingly. Peter opened the door further and slipped inside. Noose followed, standing up straight and shutting the door behind them. They were in the kitchen, the strange smell now hitting Noose's nostrils. It gave him a short, sharp shock as it transported him back to when that young woman posing as Sergeant Helen Douglas had pulled her finger out of his bum. The sweat of the embrace, the poo from his bum... *That* was the smell in this house.

Peter looked around cautiously, though much brisker than Noose. To the elder man, this companion who'd miraculously returned to life looked that much more assured. Seemingly gone was the naive speed of his younger self, to be replaced by this world-worn carelessness that gave him the impetus to just step into a murderer's house. Noose lost sight of him for a second as he stepped into the next room.

'Oh my,' came a call from the other room. Noose quickly followed, that smell intensifying. As he stepped into the living room, there was Barbara naked and strung up by her hands. A ball gag in her mouth and a thin wire around her neck, she shook her head violently as she caught sight of the two men. 'She's trying to warn us.'

'Warn us about what?'

They heard a clicking noise and looked down between Barbara's legs just in time to see a long sharp blade fire up from a small furry pink box and straight into her vagina.

'Oh fuck,' Noose yelled as blood poured from between Barbara's legs and she moaned in agony. 'We've got to get her down from there,' Noose cried out as he stepped closer. Suddenly Barbara's eyes widened as her head seemed to be pulled up straight. They noticed that the thin wire around her neck ran into a small box attached to the ceiling, which now began to pull the wire in. Tighter and tighter it got as Barbara's eyes bulged more and more. And then, along with the sound of a little cog running, the wire shot back into the box with a ferocious force and cut the woman's head clean off like it was just a piece of cheese. It dropped to the floor with a thud as her body still hung there, now quite lifeless. The two men were stunned into silence. Neither could they look at her body, nor each other. Peter stepped out of the room, his hand over his mouth, as Noose remained fixed to the spot.

The silence was soon disrupted by a thrashing at the door as it burst open and what seemed like a dozen armed police officers poured in. Peter ascended the stairs as they wrestled Noose to the floor, gasps and cries echoing the whole house as some of the officers caught sight of the horrid scene. Peter remained unmolested as he quietly lost himself in one of the bedrooms – clearly they had come for Noose, and only Noose. What a remarkable set-up, Peter thought. To those cops, Noose had been well and truly caught in the act.

* * *

Noose, his hands cuffed behind his back, was led through the

Myrtleville police station reception by two bulky cops. They needed to be bulky to hold him back when, coming in the opposite direction, was his ex-wife and son. Initially Noose didn't recognise her – her hair was white and balding, her head bent permanently to the side as the ravages of her illness had taken their toll. She sat slumped in her wheelchair, son Gary pushing her as Jacobs and Douglas walked either side. Noose was seized as he tried to get to his family, recognising his son. Gary looked back, a spiteful grin quickly forming on his face.

'You sick pervert,' Gary shouted out as Williams stormed through the double doors after them, panicking.

'What the hell's going on here? They're supposed to be in protective custody, not meeting him in reception,' she yelled at Jacobs and Douglas. The pair frowned, Jacobs pushing Gary out of the way and taking control of Sam's wheelchair as Douglas tried to put her arm around Gary. He, now a handsome young man, was as tall as his father and the spitting image of him back in the day.

'Son,' Noose cried, struggling in the tight grip of his guards and unable to look upon his ex-wife.

'I'm not your son, murderer pedophile scumbag,' Gary replied with increasing venom. Noose could no longer plead his innocence – he'd had enough. He stopped struggling and went limp, slipping from the grip of the officers and falling to his knees. 'Look what you've done to my mum, you vile worthless creature,' Gary carried on, lashing out at his dad with his foot. Williams leapt to block the kick, getting caught across her knees. She too fell as Jacobs made a grab for Gary and wrestled him away.

'What has happened to you?' Noose mumbled towards Sam, still unable to look at her. 'How did I cause this?' She remained silent, her jaw fixed shut by the disease afflicting her.

'You abandoned her, she didn't want to live anymore,' Gary yelled as Jacobs led him off. Douglas quickly pushed Sam away as Williams turned around on her knees to face Noose.

'It's not your fault, Henry,' she whispered, pausing for a moment as their eyes met. Noose sniffed away his fit of tears as she almost placed a hand on his. The officers pulled him to his feet and she too got up. 'She's suffering from a rare degenerative disease. You didn't cause that.'

'My son thinks I did,' were the last words Noose spoke as he was taken away. From that moment on he decided it best he never spoke again.

To scribble and scrape and
Untangle the trap as
Intangible taught systems
Lie unredeemed in confusion,
There appears a decision to be made -
Pour your everything.

ALEX'S RISE

Never one to normally blow his own trumpet, Alex nonetheless felt incredibly full of himself as he strode up to the Edwards' house and knocked on the door. Inside, Ruby and Arthur had spent the last few days following the news about Alex's miraculous walk-out of prison. Now, with that knock at the door, their tenuous bubble had just been burst. The blinds twitched as Alex knocked again.

'There's a crowd outside,' Ruby whispered to Arthur from the window. He, sitting on the sofa, kept his eyes fixed on the TV.

'I just don't know what overcame me,' the guard from the prison explained in an interview on the news. 'I just cannot reason why we all stood aside and let him get out.'

'Could it be he exerted some form of mind-control over you?' asked Newsman Richard Hart.

'It almost felt like I believed in him somehow, that he was doing it for me.'

Richard turned to the camera and, with the unerring devotion he'd paid to his craft for the last fifteen years, delivered in a monotonous fawn: 'Something truly remarkable is unfolding in our country. Not so very long ago we had the televised suicide of Neville Jeffries, purporting to be following the word of Peter Smith and The Great Collective. Now, Alex – the man convicted of murdering our Prime Minister – claims to be a part of this Great Collective. What is it, and how might we all reap the benefits?'

'I'll just reap what I've sown, thank you very much,' was Arthur's response, 'down on the allotment.'

Again the knock came at the door. Louder this time. 'I know you're in there,' Alex called out.

'Katie's not here,' Ruby yelled back. 'Go away.'

'I'm not here to see Katie.'

'Well we don't flippin' well wanna see you,' Arthur grunted.

'Locks cannot stop me. Open up, and an expensive repair bill can be avoided.'

At this half-hearted attempt at menace, Arthur smelt the spending of money and so leapt to his feet and rushed to the door. He unlocked it and opened it slowly. Alex walked straight in, pushing Arthur aside, and locked the door behind him.

'What do you want?' Ruby fumed, pointing her finger at the young man.

'Firstly, I want to apologise,' he said sincerely, lowering his head and looking up at the gobsmacked couple. 'I'm completely innocent, I never killed the Prime Minister.'

'To be honest, we never believed you did,' Arthur admitted, going to sit down again. 'You always were a weak sort of lad,' he carried on, putting his feet up on the sofa. Alex merely smiled at this.

'It's all a conspiracy, and I was the random fall guy they chose to stitch-up. People are beginning to believe that now.' He moved to the window and briefly looked out at the gathering followers. 'People are beginning to see that now. People are beginning to see that I speak the truth, that I can show them the way.'

'And what way is that?' Ruby wondered with frustration in her voice, 'this hocus pocus malarkey they're all spouting? The Great Collective and all that shit?'

'It is not shit, Ruby,' he replied. Ruby was a little surprised at this – after all, Alex had always addressed her as Mrs Edwards despite her encouragement to drop the formalities.

'Well, you've apologised. You can go now,' Ruby finished, taking hold of him and trying to march him to the door. He pulled himself from her grip and outstretched his hand, taking control of her body and making her step back. For a second she lost her breath, terrified at her loss of power. Arthur hadn't seemed to notice.

'I have one more thing to ask of you,' Alex continued. 'You people, my in-laws, once harboured Peter Smith in this very house.'

'Yes,' Ruby sighed. Arthur looked up and cleared his throat. 'He spread his poison through my family, just like you're trying to do now.' She felt herself released from Alex's ensconcing flow but remained fixed to the spot.

'I am not here to spread poison – I am here to warn you of his return.'

'Oh God no,' Arthur lamented, 'I thought we'd seen the last of him.'

'You were wrong. He is back, and wants to destroy me.'

'Destroy you? Why?'

'I took his place in your family.' Alex turned away from them, smiling. 'I became what he never could – your surrogate son. He is raging with anger, sick with perversion. Surely you read that book he wrote, the one Neville died for?'

'No,' Ruby uttered, stepping closer to Alex. 'But, they're saying you are like Neville, a follower of that book, part of The Great Collective.'

'That book is inconsequential – the ravings of a sick mind. I follow my own path, and want to spread only the truth.'

'Which is?' asked a confused Ruby, stepping yet closer to her son-in-law.

'That there has been too much hurt in the world,' he said quietly, turning to face his mother-in-law. 'I was framed and put inside by the hatred of Peter Smith and his suicidal followers. His book is poison, Ruby, poison.'

'You used to call me Mrs Edwards all the time.'

Alex moved in, arms outstretched, and hugged her. She embraced him. 'I never had a family of my own. I'd call you Mother, if I could,' he went on. Arthur stood up and rushed to the pair, joining in with the hugging. 'Father,' Alex whispered in his ear.

'Katie has been so distant from us for so long,' Ruby wept, her tears soaking into Alex's t-shirt. 'All we ever wanted was a loving child.'

'I love you, Mum,' Alex told her.

From then on, she was completely his.

See the sun shine, guzzle my wine.
Have a quick smoke, chewing on dope.
I can see now, clearly as night.
Opened my mind, to confusion.

Lost in big smoke, clearly confused.
Shattered image, built on misuse.
With this tight rope, wrapped round my throat.
Opened my mind, end of the line.

PETER'S ODYSSEY

Being alive does have its merits. Somebody who's been dead as many times as I have is able to say that with some conviction. In fact, everything I say is said with conviction. I've said a lot of things in my lives – some of it memorable and worthy of merit, some of it not so – and yet eventually not one single word will be remembered. Even in this current flux of apparent immortality, I will fade eventually and be gone for good with nothing to show for it. Already, there's nothing to show for it. I lost Noose to the cops again at the first hurdle, and Lucy remains dead. Yes, I keep coming back don't I! That tiresome recycling of this irksome body and life. Still, as I said, life does have its merits. One of those seemingly very few merits is the ability to experience happiness, even if it is fleeting. I can honestly say I *have* experienced brief passages of happiness. Very brief, but certain. The beauty of a woman, the scent of a flower; there is some pleasure in life. That chance, hope, of continued happiness is the ultimate goal. Now that I am returned to this previously perplexingly perverse period in my existence, I want to make a go of it. I am ready, complete – desiring the base and most important of human experience: pleasure. To clear Noose, find Lucy's murderer and stop Reaping Icon would solve all that which currently holds me back. Then, I could move on with Lauren and live out a somewhat average life. Average may seem an awkward, arrogant affront to what I could have – endless life after life and ultimate power at the helm of The Space – but once you have tasted that, you don't want to again. Trust me, the human mind is just too underdeveloped and backwards to be able to cope with such might. I want for normality, and I would hope to get it.

* * *

'You shouldn't have come here,' were the words Norman Trout managed to force through his bloodied lips. His face, coarse with age and general lack of attendance, hid just in the shadow cast by his desk lamp. Hunched next to him, I wiped the blood and snot from my own nose. We'd had quite a game of fisticuffs. 'It's got nothing to do with me.'

'Well somebody did it.'

'Yeah, Noose fucking did it,' Trout sighed, as though saddened by the apparent revelation of Noose's criminality. He crossed his head, moving it into the light. He looked desperate somehow – desperate for something I knew not. I too was desperate, and he was my reflection. I looked deep into his very being, looking for the truth. All that lay there was grey smoothness. His bent fingers grabbed at a notebook on his desk. 'I'm writing a book,' he said, smiling. 'You wrote a book, didn't you?'

'Apparently,' I responded, unsure. I certainly knew Peter Smith had written a book, but was that this Peter Smith – the man I was right now?

'I read it, I'm in it.'

'What are you after, a cut of the royalties?'

His tired eyes slid up and down as they took in my face and body with mild, quelled, annoyance. 'You come into my house, my home, pick a fight with me and accuse me of stitching that twat Noose up.' He took a deep breath, opening the notebook in his hands. 'My book is also about my life, tweaked in places like your book.'

'Tweaked in your favour.' I felt sure the book I'd been credited with wasn't in my favour. Trout just smiled.

'Hello,' he began, reading the first page of his book. 'My name is Norman Trout. I am dead.' He looked up from the book, squaring his eyes at mine. 'Metaphorically speaking.' I edged forward to try and read his book for myself. He closed it and placed it back on the desk, his hand resting on top of it. 'Because, the dead cannot actually communicate. Can they? And, your own brother as your prosecutor? Why do you feel he's prosecuting you?'

I stood up and stepped back. 'Okay, you didn't set Noose up. Someone did, I must continue my search.'

'You and that bastard destroyed me,' he yelled, grabbing hold of his book and throwing it on the floor.

'You destroyed yourself, Trout,' I calmly replied as I walked away. 'You broke the law.'

'Oh whoop-de-doo,' he screeched, getting to his feet and waving his arms in the air as I stopped in the doorway and turned back, wondering if I owed him anything. 'Call the fucking cops, why don't we? Naughty boy Norman!' He slapped his own wrist and eyed me with apparent scorn. But, there was something a little too theatrical about it. I just couldn't accept any emotional depth from this man. 'I'm just a minor, throwaway character to you, aren't I?' he carried on, 'Not even a supporting role – just a stock providing a means to an end.' He laughed. 'What's this now, eh? Is this my two page cameo in your new book? Resurrect old Norman Trout for a laugh? Well let me tell you, dick head; you're the biggest waste of a reader's time there ever was.'

'Is that so?'

'Is that so?!' he mocked, affecting a girlish voice. 'It's all in your head – you were never dead.'

I turned away and left him.

If this was the space to resurrect one-time characters from my life, then the next cameo was to be Simon Berre. The man who had, several years prior, chained me up in his office and had me beaten to within an inch of my life for meddling in his affairs had fallen on similarly hard times to Trout. He was another waste product of the justice meted out by Noose and myself – the list was potentially endless – and another possible culprit for stitching Noose up. He was not a hard man to find, having managed to somehow rebuild his construction company after we'd destroyed it. However, unlike back in the day when his rich wife had poured her dead daddy's funds into it at Simon's whim, it was now nothing more than an estate car and half a backyard. Having had a good look around said backyard, I found myself face to face with an emaciated, grey-bearded man. Stinking of booze and fags, he coughed and asked what I wanted.

'I am Peter Smith,' I told him, stepping into the light. He studied my face, puzzled.

'Am I supposed to know you?'

For a moment I actually questioned myself, wondering if it was the same man. No, this most certainly was Simon Berre. 'Don't you remember me?' He looked again, then turned away with a cough. 'Your daughter Michelle, the murders, all those years ago – I helped Inspector Noose solve the case.'

He turned back, slow and unsteady. 'Noose?' he again questioned, seemingly full of confusion. 'Michelle is dead,' he said coldly. 'She fell out of a hotel window.' He rubbed his beard. 'What do you want? After a news story?'

'I came here because Noose has been framed for murders he did not commit.'

'Like Michelle tried to frame me?'

He seemed so distant, so lost and equally carefree. His

family were gone, his business was all but gone – his brain was gone. 'Do you know anything about it?' I asked him half-heartedly, realising he probably knew little about anything. He was just another scar Noose and I had left behind.

As I stepped out of Berre's yard and onto the pavement, a figure ahead dashed behind a wall. I played dumb, walking forwards, pretending I hadn't seen them. Suddenly, as I passed, I spun around and dashed behind the wall myself. There, awaiting me, was a rather tubby timid-looking man who must have been in his late twenties. He was crouching on the ground with his back to me with his balding head provoking me to slap it as I zoned in on its lack of complexity. But, I resisted, instead hauling him to his feet and spinning him around to face me.

'Oh God,' he whined, his eyes scrunched shut. 'You're gonna beat me up now, aren't you?'

'That depends,' I replied, a flash a pleasure at his squirming replaced by shame. I let him go and he opened one eye to peek at me. 'Who are you, and why are you following me?'

'I am Justin Bates BSc.,' was his jovial response as he outstretched a hand towards mine, all his fear seemingly vanished. I shook it. 'I'm on the case of who framed Inspector Noose.'

'I see. Why?'

'Because he's innocent.'

'How do you know that?'

'Because he wouldn't have done those horrible things.' He clasped hold of the tight collar of his pink shirt and pulled at it. 'He's a good man.'

'How can you be so sure?'

'If nothing else, percentages – there have been a number of crooked cops in Myrtleville, that makes Noose more likely to be good than bad. Probability. Science dictates it.' He straightened his back. 'I have a degree… in science.'

'He could be bad by proxy,' I pointed out. Sickness can so easily spread, after all.

'Well, I have scientific evidence to prove that Noose definitely didn't do it.'

'Well why haven't you been to the police with it, and why are you following me?'

'The police never believe me, but you might.'

'Go on,' I said with some skepticism. Indeed, this man himself could have been the killer.

He fumbled in his trouser pocket and brought out a smartphone, holding it close to his face as he squinted at the screen with his fingers thrashing at it. 'I too suspected Barbara Davies as the perpetrator of the crimes, and was tracking her moves.'

'So you saw who strapped her up and killed her?' I queried with growing interest.

'Not exactly. I saw somebody exiting the house from the front a few minutes before you and Inspector Noose entered from the back.'

'Who?'

'Well I was hiding some distance away, behind a neighbour's hedge. I didn't get a close look.'

'Was it a man, a woman? Was it *you*?'

'Me? Don't be ridiculous. It was a man, but he was wearing a hood.'

'It's a start, I suppose,' I sighed.

'Well if you let me finish I will tell you my actual piece of evidence,' he shot back, waving the phone in my face and grinning proudly.

'Which is?'

'A connectivity signal for the person's phone – the one they used to wirelessly trigger the device which killed Barbara.'

'What? How?'

'Well, in layman's terms,' he smirked, 'clearly he had the

same top of the range brand phone as me, which can all link together with their own local area network. I saw him get the phone out as he walked off into the distance, and when I went on my phone's local device connection option, it was asking if I wanted to pair up with his device.' He turned the phone's screen to show me. On it read "crocbrenspear". 'We all have our own unique username.' For a moment I was puzzled, pondering over any clues this could actually give us. The Space was silent – I was treading on Noose's own toes with this one – there was no guide for me. Was I instead destined, and not Noose himself, to be the person to bring to justice the one who framed him? 'You're not thinking of taking the glory away from me, are you?' asked Justin. He snatched me from my near daydream as I re-focused my vision on him and caught a displeased look on his face. 'I can see the cogs working,' he carried on, 'like me you've worked out exactly who it is, and now you're going to toss me aside to go it alone from here.'

'You've worked out who it is?'

'Yes, it's quite easy. You mean to say you haven't?' he gloated arrogantly. He had the sort of smooth chubby face you could repeatedly punch if you didn't know any better. Sadly, I knew better. 'Inspector Noose brought his family up in Myrtleville, right?'

'Yes, what of it?'

'In Wales – crocbren is Welsh for gallows... noose.'

'Yes. And spear?' The answer came to me as I asked – an answer so horrible I just wanted to block it from reality. In some ways it was almost better that Noose *had* committed the murders all along. Gary meant spear.

I was not in want of the glory of capture. Nor was Justin. He presented the evidence to Nicola Williams, happy not to mention my name – as I'd requested – and she sent the armed squad around to arrest Noose's son. They say the surprise arrest gave his mother the fatal heart attack that sent her on her way, but in all honesty her heart must have split in two when the truth suddenly dawned on her. Besides, she had so suffered with her increasingly crippling condition. Gary Noose tried desperately to get to his mother as she slumped out of her wheelchair and came crashing to the floor in a limp mess, but the cops wouldn't allow it. He was a dangerous killer after all.

He was brought through the police station reception, where Justin tells me he came face to face with his father – the man he'd framed. Noose still just wanted to embrace his son, unable to accept the truth. Gary uttered not a single word, and nor has his father. I know that Noose now feels responsible for the murders, just as if he'd committed them himself. That his past actions towards his family could have driven his own son to do such heinous things would be something he could never recover from. As I attempt to start my own new life, I feel that Noose's is over. He may live for many more years, but the heavy shadow of these events will weigh heavy for the rest of them.

* * *

ONE MONTH LATER

'Hello Mother,' I uttered confidently as she opened the door. I couldn't quite tell what she was thinking as she squinted away the sunshine behind me – her face was too old and loose to give much away. She hobbled aside and I stepped into my home.

'And where have you been?' she asked me in a thin voice – as thin as her wiry white hair.

'Away... I've been away, Mother.' I wanted to embrace her, but that wasn't the way of our family. We kept our stilted distance, moving from the hallway into the living room and sitting down. The news was on the TV. Alex, the revolutionary new political figure, spoke of "change". Mother changed the sound to mute. My reappearance in her life *must* have been important. She did not offer me a drink. I suppose this was my home, she didn't need to offer me one. But, I felt I couldn't just help myself here anymore. This wasn't my home – I no longer felt a part of this place. I'd never felt a part of this place, if truth be told. I'd always felt like I'd crash-landed here from somewhere else – somewhere I'd never quite known, and never be able to return to. I now knew I belonged nowhere. Nobody belonged anywhere. We were all just a swathe of elements haphazardly tossed together for utter amusement – and yet, amusement for whom? Nobody was laughing. Mother most certainly wasn't laughing as she looked across at me. Slowly, but steadily, I caught a possible emotion somewhere across her face. Disappointment.

'You could have picked up the phone and called me. Leaving me alone for all these years,' she said sternly.

'Alone? What about Stuart?'

'We were so close, Peter; you and I.'

'Stuart was always your favourite,' I outright gave her, feeling I was lowering myself to these feeble human things.

'Is that what you think?' she asked angrily, her voice sharp.

'It's what I know.'

She tutted, crossing her head. 'Let us not fall out. You haven't been back five minutes.'

'I didn't come back to fall out.'

'What *did* you come back for?'

'I came back because I could.' I looked away from her. The sight of her was beginning to unnerve me. I felt something hitherto hidden – hitherto repressed – desperately clamouring to come back. Or, to remain hidden. It was agony. 'I also came back because I no longer need to hide from you. I can confront you now.'

'Hide from me?' she laughed. 'Why would you need to hide from me, your own mother?'

'I don't know.' I didn't. It was a rather foolish thing. 'I've done a lot of hiding. A lot of running away from things.'

'You're a coward, like your father. He was too afraid to even live, that's why he just upped and died. Petty man.'

'So I'm a petty coward, just like Father?'

'That's not what I'm saying at all,' she dismissed, waving a veiny hand about.

'Then what are you saying?'

'You had a lot to run from,' she mused, a brief glimmer of compassion seizing her.

'Yes, Lucy's murder for instance.' At my mention of this, she straightened her arched back and cleared her throat. 'I'd repressed the memory of that the most.'

'As well you should. We have managed to move on from that,' she said, pausing as she seemed to stop seeing. It was a difficult expression to describe, but I certainly saw it: her current vision drained, replaced by far-off recalls. 'As a family,' she finished, moving her gaze to mine.

'I must find her killer,' I told her, almost like an afterthought. 'Now that Noose has been cleared of murder.' A dreaded clamp wrapped around my chest, like there was something I really did know but had forced down so deeply that it had been lost in the abyss.

'Oh Peter, you *know* Stuart was responsible for Lucy's death. You've known all along. It was an accident – a terrible, sorry accident. It was better you forced yourself to forget it all. You and Stuart have had a very good relationship since, really.'

I *had* known all along, and I *had* forced myself to forget; so much so that I had become sick with it. Lucy had first been denied life by my own brother, and then denied justice by the family cover-up. No more of this! It was all out in the open now, and I was ready to serve up some proper vengeance for the cruel murder of an innocent young woman.

'Thank you Mother,' I said calmly as I stood up, a weight lifted from my being. I felt very good, very complete.

'Where are you going?' she cried out as I left her, the revelation suddenly dawning on her. I did not answer her. She did not deserve an answer.

I didn't quite know what to do. The flood of rage was drowning me but I just kept on walking, half knowing where my legs were taking me; to Stuart's house. What would I do to him when I arrived was anyone's guess. I, if there even was an I, was certainly complete again with not one single repression left lurking in me. Stuart would feel the full wrath of this completeness as I dished out justice on his physical form. But, then my body just stopped dead. I could move it no further, I was not in control. Was there an ebbing of my desire for destruction of my own brother? Why had I not already destroyed him, in the past, when I first became aware of his guilt before hiding it from myself? I now gave my thoughts to that past event, the full force in demonstration as I caught him weeping in his bedroom with Mother and Father by his side. He sobbed for forgiveness and pleaded not to be turned over to the police for the "mistake" he had committed. There I was, in the midst of both grief at my loss and anger at my near conviction for Lucy's murder, and now Stuart's confession was echoing through. Her killer had been my own brother, a constant rash on my existence for his arrogance and affront to it. He had taken my love, my life. I collapsed right there on the spot, seized by a self-pounding as my mind consumed itself. Never again would I remember – accept – Stuart's guilt until this day. I had been running from it, allowing him to grow and grow in his sheer indestructible flippancy. He was my prosecutor, driving me down and down until there was little more than a hollow crack of bullshit. It was as though everything that had ever happened, or would ever happen, was just crap I'd invented in my head in order to force this deeper and deeper. It *was* too horrific to fully contemplate: my own brother murdering Lucy. Again the rage built, my body moving forward once more. It was not long before I had reached Stuart's house. My hand was not my own as it bashed on the door. No reply. I found myself going around the back and breaking a window, climbing inside and hunting for him. The house was empty, I was alone.

It was some time before he came home. I had lost any concept of how long I'd been waiting, and was left relatively undisturbed in my patience. The only interference had been several unanswered calls. When Stuart walked in, alone, the energy had fully drained from me. I sat at the top of the stairs and listened as he gently sobbed to himself.

'What's the matter?' I asked instinctively from my hiding place.

'Oh my God,' he yelled, clutching his chest. He squinted up at me from the hallway below. 'Where the fucking hell have you been all these years? I thought you were dead.' He wiped away some tears with his sleeve. 'You might as well have been, you haven't missed much.'

'You seem upset.'

'Diane's left me, said I'm a waste of space.' Again he looked up at me, limply outstretching his arms towards me. I got up and walked down the stairs towards him. I couldn't quite believe it, but I found myself hugging him. His grip of me was loose. Still, this just wasn't what was done in our family. His head turned, catching sight of the answer phone light flashing. He eased away from me and pressed the button.

'You have one new message, message received today at 17:36,' the automated voice announced.

'Stuart my dear,' Mother's voice sounded from the phone,

'where are you? Guess who's back – and he remembers about Lucy.'

'It was just an accident, Pete,' he fumbled, a deep intake of breath seeming not to cease as he tried to avoid my face. 'I fancied her, you see, just brotherly jealousy. I went to see her and it all happened so quickly. She misread my actions, thought I was trying to do something horrible to her. It all happened so quickly.' He stepped slowly away from me, not turning his back, as I sorely wished this was again something I could forget and repress. But no, it would not end and I optioned my physicality to deal out pounding justice on his body. Nothing happened. I was frozen to the spot, Stuart getting further and further away until he was gone from the house. Once I felt he was far enough away, I picked up the phone and called the police. It was his turn to hide.

* * *

I was waiting for Lauren when she got home. She looked so much more vibrant and alive since Noose had been cleared. Still, the fact it was his own son who'd framed him was a difficult fact to get to grips with. The shattered mess of a man we'd been left with was also a burden on her, but she was much lighter in her step now. She smiled as she passed me and opened her fridge to get a drink out. 'You need to get a job,' were her first words to me. 'You need to start doing something with your life, settle down.'

'Settle down with you?' I replied with a wry smile. She even gave me a smile back.

'Stranger things have happened.' She poured herself some apple juice and took a sip, dropping the day's newspaper on the table in front of me. 'I feel we're all sort of turning a corner, you know?'

I looked down at the front page of the paper, the headline

reading: "ALEX WINS ELECTION!" For a brief blip I could see my long future ahead with Lauren. The perfect life full of burgeoning love. She was a woman who could give all the love in the universe to one man, and I was that man. But, she needed coaxing and allowed to blossom over time. As I stared down at Alex's haunting face below me, I knew I couldn't give her that time yet. Would I ever be able to? Reaping Icon would wreck terrible destruction on all of humanity through Alex, and I knew now that if I existed, Reaping Icon existed. To remove him would remove the sickness from the world, and in so doing I would be removing myself too.

That night I allowed myself a glimpse of the life I would likely never lead, as Lauren and I cosied up on the sofa to watch an old film. I gave in to her simple needs, her basic wants – the cuddle, the peck on the cheek. These things brought down my centuries long struggles with the madness of anger and hatred. Our slow, warm intimacy made me want to die of pure happiness right there and then. And, it was better Lauren never find out who she really was.

These are not orders,
They are observations.
Giving up your borders,
Leading to procrastinations.

Profundity in abundance,
Everyone has their five minutes.

ALEX'S ISSUES
(PART ONE)

'It's a happy day for me… a very happy day,' Alex revelled.

'It's a happy day for us all, Leader,' replied one of his doting minions, rubbing his eye. They were just mindless means to an end in both Alex's opinion and in reality.

'Yes, now I'm in a position to deal with all the sickness I see in society.'

'Society's ills are a major concern.'

'So much illness. So much pain and suffering.' Alex walked over to the large mirror on the wall. The fireplace below was glossy and grand, but being gas with fake coals made it less appealing to him. Anyway, it was off. He tried to look at himself, but he couldn't see anybody. However, he'd come here so now he felt he had to stay for a while. The minion was also faceless; just a bland yawn of a man awaiting instructions to do something ineffectual. No, Alex had other ideas – ideas he would command from the safety of this office. He was the new Leader, and he would most certainly lead. Lead into misery. 'So much…' Alex uttered, pausing to think up the correct word. And then, Katie entered his mind. 'Perversion.' He smiled, hoping to see it in the mirror. There was nothing to see. 'Our traditional values have been twisted and perverted,' he carried on, as though formulating some imminent policy off the top of his head.

At that moment, Ruby walked in from a little side door.

Apron on, and duster in hand, she casually went about her business of ridding the room of dust. Well, moving it about. The static grab of the duster was slack, most of it simply shifting about in miniature whirlwinds as the operator of the duster whistled and hummed happily to herself. Arthur soon appeared too, pushing a vacuum cleaner. He slowly set about uncoiling the cable and looking for a free plug socket. Alex cleared his throat to get their attention, but they just carried on regardless. He did it again, more pronounced, and Arthur looked across.

'You want to get a pack of lozenges for that throat, lad,' Arthur remarked.

'Get your lackey to pop out for some,' Ruby added, pointing at the suited minion with her duster. She narrowed her eyes at the glaring man. 'Looks like he's slacking to me.'

The minion suddenly looked on edge, fiddling with his tight collar and rubbing at his eye yet again as Alex focused his attention on him too. Ruby obviously felt she held some sway in this place, and that was enough for Alex to allow her to hold it. It amused him somewhat to think of this silly insignificant man working up a sweat over an old cleaning woman's vague implications. Then again, why shouldn't the man sweat? He'd spent his whole life crawling and tugging at the hem of wealth and power. Alex had just shot straight to the top within a matter of weeks. An act worth applauding. This snivelling suckling in front of the amazing Alex right now was all too willing to pay lip service in his continuing struggle to reach the top; but it must have frustrated him to some degree when he compared his own ongoing journey. He'd spent his entire life taking one step forward and two steps back, but he'd just about managed to reach his position in the offices of power. He'd been here a while, having dealt with the previous prime minister; and now had to crawl around 'The Leader'. In many ways this was his office more than it was Alex's – in his own mind, at least. And now the new crew were in, doing as they pleased and headed by the quick man who could rise up from obscurity to the most powerful position in the country in a flash. Still, the man certainly was a doting minion. Though a part of him grew more and more angry at Alex's speedy rise, he was still in awe. It had been a superb feat, and this was still the honeymoon. The Leader could do no wrong at present. Well, with Reaping Icon in bodily form, he would *never* do any wrong… if there was nobody to stop him. It took a certain type of person to stop Reaping Icon – not that Reaping Icon had ever been stopped before. You fight evil with evil – even when the first evil is just quelling other evil to begin with. The minion knew nothing of Reaping Icon, and that was how it was to remain. Alex's label was The Leader, and his rise was purely of his own doing – officially. There was much awe surrounding him. He had that affect on people now. All he'd have to do was think about how he wanted somebody to feel about him, and they would. It wouldn't be an altogether full or ongoing feeling, but it was enough to create the buzz necessary to do as he wished. The Space was at his whim, just a malleable tool to ease the task at hand. Nothing more.

'Something wrong with your eye?' Ruby asked the man as she and Alex kept on with their intense staring.

'No, no, not at all,' he stuttered, trying not to rub as he twitched. 'Just an eyelash in my eye, it's gone now.'

Ruby dismissed him with a flick of the duster, and he dashed, overwhelmingly relieved, from the room. She now turned to Alex as Arthur went about vacuuming the crimson carpet. 'So what are your plans now, oh Leader?!' she chuckled over the noise.

He smiled back, but did not reply. Ruby didn't need an answer, she needed nothing. She already had everything she'd ever wanted.

Give me a reason,
Supply more than goods.
I am gripping,
On tenterhooks.

THERE'S AN EYELASH IN MY EYE

There's an eyelash in my eye, and it's driving me crazy. I've been trying to get it out for over an hour now, and it just won't come. I've tried everything from rinsing my eye out to just plain rubbing it, and I'm fresh out of ideas. My eye is getting pretty sore now, and no matter what I do it is so irritating. I don't know how much more of this I can take. The longest I've ever had an eyelash in my eye for in the past is about five minutes. Even that felt like an age. Usually, with a bit of rubbing and rinsing, it comes out. Sometimes I can even see the eyelash floating around in there if I look in a mirror and pull my bottom eyelid down. Not this time, no! This time is the worst eyelash in my eye incident I've ever had. I suppose you have to laugh, really, that it's been going on for over an hour and I probably will laugh once I have it out. What to do next, though? I've gone right around the houses with methods to get it out, so the only thing to do is try them all again. It's getting so, so sore now that it really isn't much of a laughing matter at all. In fact, it's more of a crying matter. I haven't cried in a long time, but this situation certainly warrants tears. I'll blow my nose and see if that gets the damn thing out. Another rinse too, and that might just do it. Oh God, I look so awful. Here I am, silently screaming as I plead with my own reflection to help me out. If I can't do anything myself, what is my reflection going to do? This is madness, I'm talking to my own reflection now! Those sort of people are crackers, aren't they? Talking to yourself is just a self-indulgent waste of time. Still, that's what

I've always thought up until maybe right this very second as I'm doing just that. Here I am, the man with the fucking eyelash in his eye and it's getting more and more painful as the time passes. It must be well over an hour by now. I should really have kept a tab on when I first felt the eyelash, then I'd know the exact time wouldn't I? I suppose the reason I didn't make a note of the time is because usually an eyelash in my eye never lasts more than a few minutes. I really should have made a note of the time, then I'd have a record of this bizarre, rather horrible event. I shouldn't swear, but fuck it! This kind of pain truly does warrant lots of swearing. It's difficult to explain the pain. It's almost like a culmination of every possible pain there is, but compressed down and focused on a small body part. There's a bit of drowning as I get short of breath because I'm so worked up, and a bit of stabbing as I jab my bloody eye. I almost feel like I'm on fire with the searing throb of the rubbed eye. Bloody hell, I'm going mad standing here trying to sort this out. I've got so much work to do, I can't afford to have this bastard eyelash in my eye. It's ruining my day. No, it's ruined my day. No matter how long it now takes to get out – it could pop out right now, or take another hour – this day will go down in history as the day I had the worst eyelash in my eye ever! Oh God imagine it, another hour of this! I think I'd have to kill myself before I let another hour pass in this condition. This isn't living, it's not even existing. I feel like I'm caught in some kind of purgatory between life and death. It is sheer torment, like an everlasting hell with no let-up. No, it's not even like a state between life and death; that would be far more tolerable. This kind of annoyance goes far beyond any kind of comparison. It is unbelievably beyond anything else yet suffered by the entire history of life on any planet anywhere in the universe. I'm babbling, I'm off my head! Look, just calm down and let's get this out of my eye once and for all. If I just settle my breathing and think logically about this, I can sort it all out and my life can go back to normal. I've got all this work to do; nobody else is going to do it are they?! And, nobody else here has got an eyelash in their eye either, have they? I'm all alone in here, nobody has been in to check if I'm alright. Nobody cares about me having an eyelash in my eye. It's not like cancer, or a heart attack is it? I should count my blessings really, I'm very lucky I haven't got cancer. Still, my eye is throbbing now with this irritant in it and to all intents and purposes I could very easily have a massive inoperable brain tumour pummelling at my eye from behind. At this exact moment in time, right now, I could be seconds from its explosion inside my brain. My head is just milliseconds from popping like an over-inflated balloon. The mirror I'm looking at would be home to the splattered goo that remained of my face. Maybe my face would look better as mere goo, because at the moment it looks dreadful. I can't quite see that it is my face because I'm losing vision in one eye. The other is straining to see but it can't quite make anything out now. Maybe it's all in my head, a desperate attempt to detach myself from this body as that twat of an eyelash does its evil bidding from my eye. Maybe there is no eyelash in my eye at all, and it's all a figment of my imagination? Would my imagination be so cruel as to do that to me? To itself? I don't feel myself at all anymore, even though my life has been pretty good of late. There were simply no worries whatsoever in my life up until just over an hour ago. I've got a lovely partner, well-paying high-powered job; the works. What have I done to deserve an eyelash in the eye? No, I really should count my blessings. When this torment is all over, my life will go back to the way it was before. I might be behind with my work, but there are mitigating circumstances. Alex will understand when I explain that I had an eyelash in my eye. Everyone has experienced that, surely? I'm not so sure they have. Nobody could have experienced this prolonged level of injustice and survived to tell the tale. Then again, it is no tale. I'm not going to just turn this into some sort of after dinner comical anecdote and cheapen the frustration and horror. Oh, listen up my friends, I spent several hours weeping in agony as I struggled to get an eyelash out of my eye! What a complete and utter tosser I'd sound. Perhaps my friends already see me as a tosser and an anecdote about my suffering wouldn't make much of a difference to their opinions of me? I really should ask them what they actually think of me. Right now I reckon I could ask anyone anything, and say whatever I wanted to say. I could walk straight up to a crazed lunatic pointing a loaded gun at me, put my lips around it, and tell him to go to hell. I can do anything right now, except get this eyelash out of my eye. I'm completely powerful and completely powerless all at the same time, able to conquer the greatest evil yet brought to my knees by an eyelash in my eye. Yes, here I am on my knees now, with my head in my hands crying like a little git. Nobody could care in the slightest about my pain, could they? They let it all wash over their heads as my eye pulsates with greater and greater ferocity. How would they like it? How would they like to suffer as I am? Maybe I should gouge my eye out and force it into their skull to let them feel the pain! See how they like it! They're all laughing at me, I know it. Everybody in the entire world is roaring with laughter at the stupid little git on his knees in the bathroom. No, let's get up. Pull yourself together, you fool! Nobody is laughing at me, are they? Although, I can kind of hear laughter. If I stay silent long enough, suppress even the voice in my own head, I can just about make out a distant giggling. Is it for my benefit, or is there something else going on that I don't know about? I don't know about anything now, I'm completely broken and finished. This is so utterly spirit-breaking for me. Nonsense, I'm not dying, I've only got an eyelash in my eye. Only? Do people not know how painful it is?! It is agony, the pain of a million tropical diseases rolled into one syringe and injected directly into my pupil. This is madness, madness, madness! I need to laugh about this, laughter is the best medicine! Haha, oh how funny it is to have an eyelash in my eye causing me so much grief. There isn't even a window in here for me to look out of or get some fresh air. I'd never noticed that before now. All I'd done was shoot in and out of here for a piss or a poo, never giving the actual room any consideration at all. I now know everything there is to know about this room. Or do I? Maybe now I know there's no window in this room it proves I know even less about here than I did before? I know nothing at all about anything, all the information I've seemingly clung onto so easily in life now pouring out of me and speeding away down the drain. I need some fresh air, badly. I can't get any in here, I'm closed in as the walls tower above and close in. But, I can't go out there and seek any oxygen; if I do, I'll be exposing myself to all and sundry to be made the laughing stock of the entire office. I'll never live this down, never be able to regain any kind of respect ever again. Forever I will be the little git who was brought crashing to his knees by an eyelash in his eye. That'll never do, I can't be that person in their eyes. I must retain the impression they already have of me. Well, the impression I think they have of me. For all I know I'm already the idiot who gets brought down by an eyelash in his eye. I'd never given it much thought before today, never before pondered much upon what people thought of me. If anything, having this eyelash in my eye has made me see more clearly than I have ever done before. I'm beginning to see people for who they really are, beginning to see what they really think of me. It is not pretty, but it is truth and truth is far more honest than what went before it. This eyelash in my eye has changed everything, it is the beginning of the rest of my life. It will reshape who I am and what I think. Hello again, face! My eye is really bloodshot now, but that doesn't matter. The pain and sight of it is such a small payment to make for the clarity it is delivering me. It's giving me time to think now, for possibly the first time in my entire life. Do I really like my job? I certainly don't like the people I work with. They're all horrible, horrible people with sad little lives who just go on and on about the same things over and over again. I hate that, I can't stand their self-obsession. It is not me at all, I am not like them in any possible way. And, Alex is the worst of the lot. The Leader? How pompous. Such a liar and a cheat, and the most idiotic person you could ever come across. That he could possibly think himself fit to lead anyone, let alone me, is anyone's guess. I should be The Leader, he has no right to tell me what to do. And then there's my partner! Hah, that's the biggest joke of the lot. If there's anything more irritating than an eyelash in the eye, it's her and her constant moaning and telling me what to do. If anything, I've kind of got caught up in the whole thing. I never wanted to go out with her, I just wanted a girlfriend because everyone else had one. It's gone on far too long now though, it's too late to back out of it now. Everything has gotten ever so serious, with our families merging and us living together. There's so much talk of a wedding, I just don't know what she has planned for my life. Just like this eyelash, it's never me who plans my life; everything is laid out in front of me in the order they want it to happen. There is the set path I must follow, and God forbid I deviate from it! In fact, the more I actually think about it, my life has been one long torment in which this eyelash saga is just the latest attack. I must be thankful that the rogue eyelash has afforded me this insight. It has been delivered from some higher being with the purpose of forcing me to see where my life has been going wrong. I will not ignore this opportunity to start afresh and alter things for the better. I have been gifted with a second chance by the eyelash, it is wise and all-knowing! Now I know I have lost the plot. An eyelash with higher powers? I've flipped my lid. Is it any wonder I'm going out of my head in here with this awful eyelash in my eye? So many rinses, so many blows of the nose, and still nothing. If I rub it any more I'm afraid I'm going to start punching it. I could just grab a pen out of my jacket pocket and stab the fucker. Stab myself right in the eye, pull it out and flush it down the toilet! That would serve it right for not flushing out this eyelash by itself. Does my eye want me to suffer? Is it punishing me on purpose? Perhaps I have looked upon something that I shouldn't have in the past, and this is my penance. I've done no wrong in my life, I've caused no suffering to anyone. Except myself, probably. This is yet another opportunity for my own body to make me suffer, push me to the edge of fragility and watch me teeter like a helpless baby starved of its mother's milk. I could do with a drink, actually, but again I cannot leave this room until the eyelash is out. I'd drink my own damn piss if it meant the eyelash would come out. What then, though? I fear the time after the eyelash has come out, it represents the next stage of my life; the stage where I must make good my decision to change things. As long as the eyelash remains in my eye, so does my current set of circumstances. I just cannot believe it! I blinked really hard and it's gone, vanished from my eye! The torment has disappeared, I am free from the eyelash's reign of tyranny. Hurrah, huzzah, oh how silly I have been. I didn't mean any of what I said, my life is fine as it is and I was just worked up is all. I can leave the bathroom happy in the knowledge that I just had a brief blip in my life, just a flash of the darkness that has thankfully not befallen me before. You must be fucking joking, I've got to the door and blinked heavily again – it's back, worse than ever before! There's an eyelash in my eye, and it's driven me crazy.

You remember, you were inside,
And the Devil knows -
You gotta hide from me.

ALEX'S ISSUES
(PART TWO)

Alex was alone for the first time in a long while. He looked alone, and he felt alone. He washed his hands and looked in the bathroom mirror. Still he couldn't see himself. There was absolute space ahead – endless and never beginning all at once. He decided that if Reaping Icon would go away, he'd be able to see himself again. Did he want to see himself? It didn't matter, because Reaping Icon wasn't going anywhere. They were one now.

He thought about Emma – he should have just been a man and gone off with her instead of marrying Katie. What a fool. Never mind, it was done now and Katie would pay for her crimes. Alex had allowed hate to flood in; hatred in its most basic form. Katie found sexual fulfilment with other women. 'A perversion,' Alex said to himself. He stared longingly at the mirror. It would not reflect his image. It was not playing ball. 'Perversion must be stamped out.'

* * *

'Prime Minister,' Newsman Richard Hart addressed Alex.

'Leader – please, Richard, address me as Leader,' Alex interrupted.

'Very well, Leader-'

'Because we as a country need a leader, a guiding force for

good. Ill health has crept in to our society. It must be cured,' Alex again interrupted, feeling no need to smile as he turned to face the camera with a vexed crease to his otherwise line-free face.

Richard cleared his throat, shuffling some paper props on the sofa between them as he gauged whether or not Alex was going to continue talking. He did not. Instead, he kept his glare focused on the camera. 'Surely, if we as a nation are sick, then an alias such as Doctor would be more fitting?'

'I will guide the nation towards the doctors and nurses who will aid in my cure.'

'And what specifically are these illnesses, and indeed cures?'

'Oh Richard,' Alex groaned, turning to face his interviewer, 'knowing is the first step. If you don't know, you cannot help in the recuperation.'

'That's why I asked.'

Their eyes met, and at once Richard was fully immersed in Alex's ocean. There was no flapping, no clamouring to get out; he had no possible idea he had been taken in. Alex was simply too good at what he was doing.

Cut myself off from the world,
Contemplate my narcissistic ways.
I'm not a hero, I deny myself that honour.
I'm a blank canvas, mould what you wish of me.

Nobody wants me to just
Do whatever I want.
A feeling that they might change me
And leave something behind.

NOOSE'S DILEMMA

It was the first time he'd been out in a while. He didn't know exactly how long it had been and, furthermore, didn't care. He didn't care about anything. Once he'd reached the end of the street, it suddenly dawned on him that he *was* outside. He wasn't even fully aware of where he'd been staying, or how he'd been eating and drinking. He was still physically alive, so he must have been eating something. His weight had dropped significantly, however, and he was literally a shadow of his prior self. Grey-skinned, gaunt and hunched; the pathetic thing shuffled along with no particular reason to do so only that he hadn't done so for a while. This shadow would have had its own shadow too, but for the fact the sun was as far away from this place as it could get. He passed a billboard with the headline "HOMOSEXUALITY OUTLAWED" written on it, but he'd either not seen it or it hadn't gone in because he kept on unperturbed. People walked by in silence, nobody seeming to take the blind bit of notice of the billboard or Noose – like neither were worth bothering with. There seemed to be enough going on for them without having to take either of these two things on as well. Only one person seemed interested in Noose, and only momentarily, as they whipped their smartphone out and made a quick recording of the stooped wreck as he hobbled along. 'I'm sure it's him,' were their only words, before they moved on, flicking through their other photos and videos. One video on the phone showed a man being kicked and punched in the middle of the street as passers-by stood and watched, most of them holding up their phones to take pictures and record the event as well. 'Dirty queer fucker,' one of the attackers yelled, before the viewer swiped to his next video.

Noose couldn't look up to the sky, though the dull day could have told him it was full of clouds. Even so, he couldn't look up because of his bent neck. The tragedy of his life had not only destroyed him mentally but taken an irreversible toll physically too. He also knew not to look up to the sky – it was one less place to find the face with the smirk looking at him. He knew who's face it was now. Well, he thought he knew. He'd decided it was his own face, the face of the man who he should have been. The Henry Noose who he could have been had he done the right things in his life was constantly watching him and smirking, appearing first on the carpet at the police station and since then as far as behind his own eyelids. Or as close. He couldn't escape the vision of the man he could have been had he not done wrong to his wife and child. That child had become such a vile monster, and it was all Noose's fault. That's what he believed, anyway, and everybody had given up trying to convince him otherwise. In fact, a great number of people hadn't even bothered to try to convince him at all. It was both easier to believe that Noose had actually contributed to his son's crimes and ignore him altogether. It certainly looked like Father was to blame for both Nurture *and* Nature.

He wanted to play things over in his mind to try to make sense of them, but the memories just weren't there. He couldn't even fully recall the brief altercation he and Gary had at the police station just after Barbara's murder. He knew the lad had blamed him for the state Sam was in, but that was about it. That wasn't enough to go on; enough to create a whirlwind of pain in his brain. He was just fully burnt out now. To think that Gary had killed Barbara less than an hour before dashing down to the station and putting on that performance… terrible.

'Noose,' a voice called out ahead of the man. He hadn't

heard it. 'Noose,' came the call again. It was Peter. Suddenly Noose bumped into him and twisted his tilted head to look up. 'You look a state,' Peter pointed out, nearly pleased with his honesty. Noose just stared at him. 'Still not speaking?' Peter went on, a playful cadence in his speech. 'You need to get a grip. Terrible things happen, that's life. I've realised that. Nothing we can do about it.'

'We can kill ourselves and escape,' was the former inspector's husky words.

'You could,' Peter laughed, 'but it didn't work for me.'

'I deserve to stay alive and suffer some more,' Noose mumbled, trying to push Peter out of the way to move on. He was weak, Peter would not let him by. 'So Stuart murdered Lucy.' It was now Noose's turn to laugh. 'And you just forgot about it until now?'

'I don't know if there's any way back for us, Noose, I really don't,' Peter said with any trace of forced humour gone. 'Certainly not me, anyway. I could have made something with Lauren, but it's just not to be.' He looked over at the billboard sign.

'Well I'm finished with everyone, I just couldn't give a shit about anything anymore.'

'That's too bad, because I need your help... one last time.'

'What this time, Peter? Your botty need wiping, does it?'

'Reaping Icon, Noose; I'm the only one who can stop Reaping Icon, but to do that I then need someone to stop me. Only you can stop me.'

'And why should we stop Reaping Icon, exactly? I'm not a complete fool, I see what this is all about.' Noose straightened his back as much as he could to square up to Peter. 'Let the human race burn, my boy. I'm done helping people. All it got me was hell. And why should you want to help people anymore?'

'I don't know,' was Peter's honest response. Noose had a

valid point. 'I guess we should just wallow in self-pity.'

'Go and have your life with Lauren, hide yourself away and forget about everyone else.'

'If I do that I'll just keep coming back. If I stop Reaping Icon, at least I'll have a relatively normal life once. Then, all this can stop.'

'And why do you need my help? How am I the only one who can stop you?'

'You are the closest non-collective link I have. You have been like a father to me. Our emotional attachment will break through the tirade Reaping Icon will reign down on my mind.'

There was the first glimmer of an emotion other than tepid anger from Noose as he edged back from Peter. 'Like a father? I couldn't even be a father to my own son,' he coughed, trying to hold back.

'You couldn't help your son, Noose, but you can help me,' Peter pleaded, getting hold of the feeble man and pulling him closer. 'Be the one to set me free from The Space's curse.'

Noose managed to shake away from Peter's grip and turned away. 'I'll think about it,' he responded coldly, shuffling off back down the street. Peter didn't go after him. He knew that hassling Noose wouldn't solve anything. He turned and left the former inspector to wander on. Wander on he did – just going on and on until his feet could no longer carry him. He collapsed in a heap, famished and only semi-conscious as his vision caught a bright glow ahead. An angel – both a part of the light and emerging from it – swooped down and swept Noose off his feet, carrying him beyond all possible harm. Only vague features of hers formed in his sight: her melted brown eyes, her perfect bob of a haircut. The hair was pale, shiny, though could once have been dark. She was as old as Noose and yet timeless in her wrinkle-free features. She had lived and loved, fought and fretted. She was Nicola Williams.

Noose wakened one day to find himself feeling rather good. He was comfortable, he was relaxed. The room was warm and breezy at the same time, no stifle of airlessness or brightness of intense false lighting. Only the morning sun lit the room, though he couldn't see much of the room from within the four-poster bed. Soft silk netting surrounded him, and the duvet on top of him also had a rich silk feel. He felt itchy for a second, scratching his naked leg as it slipped out from beneath its covering. If this was death, it was pretty good. His last memory was of seeing an angel coming to take him away from that horrible, horrible planet full of horrible, horrible people and that felt like so long ago now.

'Terrible things are happening,' a voice suddenly called out from beside him, 'and I have to enforce them. They're the law.' Noose knew the voice. It was Nicola. He didn't want the comfort to end, so just carried on lying there next to her. She placed her hand on his chest and he couldn't recoil. He didn't want to recoil. 'For God's sake Henry, when will you just be right again?' she sighed, kissing his chest. He felt her naked breast press against his side as she slipped a leg on top of his. He didn't want to be right, he just wanted to hide away from everything and be nursed by a beautiful woman. Nicola certainly was beautiful, and he'd never been able to resist her. That's what destroyed his marriage, turned his son into a psychotic maniac. He didn't care about that anymore. Everything was nothing to Noose now; it was just easier that way. 'What do you think of this new gay law?' she asked him, but he would not be shaken from his inward fix. He just smiled as she lifted her head to study his face and push for a reply. She couldn't antagonise him, he was indestructible now he'd fallen so completely.

The wildest notion of nonsense there ever was,
Intersections of promise and utility -
Unfolding and consuming
As never before.

But everything has happened already,
Nothing can be new that will occur -
All on shuffle and repeat
Just as before.

THE EMPTY MIRROR

There was always paperwork. Paperwork, paperwork, paperwork. Even when you've swooped into power so quickly and efficiently as Alex – with all his peculiar airs and graces – there is still paperwork to be done. He didn't want to have to read and sign these things. He just wanted to breeze through the entire experience in a swoosh of destruction. And, he could easily achieve it that way. But, Alex was just Alex, from Reaping Icon's point of view. To be Peter Smith, with his near complete connection to The Space, would allow such smoother sliding into devastation. Not that humanity needed much sliding. A shave of gliding and be done.

Alex was sitting there at his desk with a big pile of stuff to go through, when one of his cabinet ministers knocked on the door. Alex knew who was knocking, and indeed why he was knocking. Calling him in casually, Alex yawned a little and stretched his arms into the space above his head. 'Yes, Eddie?' he addressed the man with indifference as his arms fell back to the desk.

'Leader,' Eddie opened, standing just inside the door as it sealed behind him. Alex pushed the papers away and stood up, walking over to the large mirror on the wall. He'd given up looking at, or indeed for, himself and simply bent down to the fireplace below. Turning the knob to release the gas, and pressing the ignition button, the fire came to life and started burning through the fake coals. Alex stood straight, looking down at the faux open fire with disappointment. There was even a sharp metal poker on a stand by the fire in which to stoke it. Stoke a pretend fire? It was perhaps this that annoyed Alex more than anything else right now. Ludicrous pomp was how he saw it, some kind of wannabe act lacking the effort to make that extra step necessary for a real open fire. 'I must speak with you,' Eddie carried on.

'Must you?' Alex replied, yet again yawning, as he fingered the poker momentarily.

'Yes. It's about this homosexuality thing,' Eddie said nervously. Alex picked the poker up and held the tip over the searing flames of the fire below him.

'You're gay, aren't you Eddie?'

He cleared his throat. 'Yes.'

'Drop your trousers and underpants, Eddie,' Alex instructed him calmly. Suddenly, Eddie was overcome with suffocating terror. He felt as though he was deep, deep down and bound so completely. In turn, he thought he could see Alex flailing in front of him, but he was still holding the poker over the fire. 'I shan't ask again, Eddie.'

The tormented man could not fight the meld of Reaping Icon, and he dropped his trousers and underpants. They lay cumbersomely around his ankles as he found himself turning his back on Alex and bending over the desk. Then came the most unimaginable atrocity to humanity as a whole – the suffering of one single being – as Alex forced the red hot poker up Eddie's anus.

* * *

Alex was staring into the fire when Ruby and Arthur walked in. They stood near the door, Ruby looking over at the desk and the brown stain on the carpet beside it as Arthur fixed his sight on Ruby. He felt he couldn't look at Alex right now, though he didn't know why.

'There's cleaning to do,' Alex uttered to the pair.

'So I can see. I, we, heard the screams,' Ruby replied. 'Is it true?'

'Is what true?'

'What we heard about Eddie,' Ruby clarified bravely. Now Arthur looked across at Alex.

'What did you hear about Eddie?'

'That he just died in here.'

Alex smiled and looked up into the mirror. All he could see was Ruby and Arthur – there was no sign of himself in the reflective surface. 'It was a terrible accident.' Alex turned to face the pair. 'He was gay, you see. He couldn't cope with being a criminal any longer.' He wanted the pair to step closer, and they did. Their bodily control was overruled as they lost all control and just had to get closer to Alex. He stayed perfectly rigid, though loose somehow, and spoke again once the pair were within an inch of him: 'You're not a fan of gays, are you?' he asked them.

'Of course not,' was Ruby's quick response, little thought behind it. She wasn't here to think. Was anybody?

'Turns my stomach,' Arthur spoke.

'I thought as much,' Alex enthused, instantly allowing the pair from his mental hold and instead embracing them physically. The three hugged, Ruby feeling truly whole. She was all too willing to sponge Eddie's blood up off the carpet now. 'For the first time in my entire life, I'm truly happy,' Alex whispered in their ears.

'What about when you married our daughter?' Ruby whispered back. Not really requiring an answer.

'There was always something wrong with her.'

'Yes. We know what you mean.'

* * *

Alex was alone, just standing there in his office with an empty mirror for company. He didn't need company – no human could provide what he wished for now. He was both Alex and Reaping Icon in one, and needed nothing from any mere human. Humanity as a whole, on the other hand, could provide just what he most desired – total destruction. That way, suffering could actually end. It was a means to an end.

He focused his mind on Peter; drawing him close, winding the cord up. He was fully prepared for the time when Peter *would* come for him, and it was all known to him. He was Reaping Icon, and he knew everything. Even if he was in such a weak-minded body as Alex, he was still more powerful than any other individual currently on this pathetic blue-green planet. More powerful, bar one: Peter Smith. And yet, Peter was not so much an individual as an amalgamation of dozens of past, present and future lives clutching precariously onto an undesirably endless timeline. Reaping Icon knew exactly how to deal with Peter Smith. It was going to be very easy.

Clearance has been given to raid the fridge,
But there's nothing of note to consume.

CONTEMPLATION

Peter wanted to kiss the birthmark on Lauren's neck. He wanted to kiss all of her body. But, doing so was proving difficult. He knew this was possibly the last time he would spend the night at her flat, and he wanted her to just let go and give in to her carnal desires. However, this was Lauren, and she was never going to just do that. This was one of the most alluring things about the woman. She could so easily resist that which others desperately sought out. But why? Was she some kind of asexual bore? Peter certainly didn't think so – after all, he had pursued her for all this time. And was that precisely why he pursued her – the knowledge, and hope, that she *would* resist and keep the full spectrum of intimacy at bay? That was for Peter to know (or work out) and nobody else.

They had spent the last three hours discussing The Space. Peter had opened up fully to her, telling her everything. It had been a cathartic release for him, and for her she had been able to finally consume who Peter really was. The sheath, the facade – all had fallen away and the pair had reached the perfect point of connection. She had been able to absorb The Space's concept and existence so easily, so fluidly, and it was this that drew Peter in even more.

She was almost asleep now, and was starting to feel a bit heavy. Peter eased himself from beside her, watching as she curled up on the sofa without him. He stood up and walked over to the kitchen. There was going to be no sexual contact with Lauren tonight, and he knew that tomorrow he was going to confront Alex. He checked his watch: 10pm. In a way he no longer even yearned for the sexual. He was beyond that now, and he had to stand back from Lauren... from everyone. No longer was he a part of humanity. Permitting himself one final look at the impenetrable one, he exited.

* * *

Anna Davies was nervous to go to the door. It was gone 11pm now and the doorbell went again. She'd lost everything already, save her own life, and letting in whoever was at the door wasn't really going to hurt her. She could lose her own life and not care right now. If you could even call it a life. It didn't matter to her. So, she opened the door. There stood Peter Smith, the man she was convinced had murdered her daughter all those years ago. That his brother Stuart had actually done the deed had not eased her hatred of this fiend who now stood in front of her. If anything it made her despise Peter even more. Her daughter's murder had been the Smith family secret – the big joke to share and laugh about over the dinner table. Oh how she wished for the whole family to rot in damnation.

Peter just stood there, hoping to come up with a reason why he'd come to see the mother of the one he'd lost. No reason was forthcoming. She looked back at him, stooped but keen to display firmness. He knew she was a pale wreck of her former self, and it destroyed him to think his own brother had left all this in his wake. Now he wished he hadn't come, but felt the overriding need to resolve something. Anything.

'Can I come in?' he asked her, thinking it would at least give her some choice and control over the situation. To bring her to her ease was all that could be done at present. And, to his surprise, she stood aside. He stepped in.

'It was so long ago now, and yet it feels so new and so raw,'

Anna said coldly, unable to sit in Peter's presence. Instead she supported her weight against the kitchen units, next to the knife drawer.

'I think about Lucy every day.'

'Do you?' she came back at him, doubting. 'Do you really?' Peter looked away sheepishly. He knew he hadn't thought about her every day. He'd blocked her from his mind for years. 'I reached the limit of thinking I could cope with. I stopped thinking,' she told him. He knew where she was coming from. 'And all this time, with you walking around a free man and me knowing for sure that you'd done it.'

'It was Stuart, not me.'

'It doesn't really matter now, does it? It doesn't matter which one of your family did it. Lucy was murdered, there's no altering that.' She opened the knife drawer and took one out, studying the blade as she waved the object in front of her. Peter sat up, taking a deep breath. 'A human life is so easy to do away with. My husband found that out when he ended his own.'

'Please, Anna, don't do anything foolish.'

'We could both die by this simple knife tonight, couldn't we? Rid the world of our miserable existences.'

Peter got up and walked confidently up to her, taking the knife. She did not resist. In a way, she sighed with relief, ready for him to do away with her so that she didn't have to. But, he put it back in the drawer and held both her hands. He too felt relief, crying as her hard face softened. 'I loved your daughter, Anna,' he told her. He may well have loved her, though he couldn't be certain. But still, this was what Anna needed to hear. 'And, she loved me back.' She too broke into a sob. 'I will find Stuart, and bring him to justice. He will pay,' he finished.

That suddenly filled her with dread. Bringing to justice her daughter's murderer would mark the end of two decades of her life's focus. Where would she go from here? Where *could* she go? That would be that. Finished. Peter felt like a bad actor, playing his part quite well but being very conscious of the fact he was playing. He'd come to the end of his repertoire, too, and just wanted to bolt. He couldn't very well up and leave immediately, and thought to occupy his mind on anything that would fill it before a reasonable enough time had elapsed to allow a respectable exit. That in itself seemed like enough to fill his mind.

He thought of his original life, lived hundreds of years ago, when The Space had first presented itself to the group of 'higher minds' he belonged to. The Great Collective were just conjurers, witches even; people who had come together to search for the limits of human achievement and been forced to gather in secret because of persecution. In a way they probably deserved persecution – pompous, arrogant people. Years, and lives, had passed; but humanity hadn't. Peter had seen it all – what people feared and hated may have shifted slightly, but not fearing and hating itself. That would always remain. He could see that, and it made him indifferent. Here he was all this time later, bogged down with people in a trapped cycle that could be left to run and run. Sitting watching TV with Mother was always just around the corner. He was alive all this time, yet he felt dead.

* * *

'I had feelings for him once,' Emma told Peter. 'Romantic feelings.'

'And for Katie?'

'What about Katie?' Emma snapped, defensive. She remembered Peter as the nosy lodger of the Edwards household, and was never very fond of him.

'I can quite easily read you, Emma,' Peter replied measuredly.

'And?'

'You and Katie had a dalliance or two – sexually speaking.'

'What?!' Emma cried out, her eyes darting about as she fidgeted with her bushy dark hair.

'Look, you're well aware of what Alex is up to now with this law he has passed. He's done it because of what happened in his life, the people who affected him.'

'So it's my fault?' Emma snapped.

'No.' Peter tapped his chin, thinking fast. He knew he was most certainly coming across as a creepy sort of figure to this beauty, but he didn't care. He had his goal, and he would reach it. 'Look, Alex isn't himself, he's been possessed as it were by a horrible weight. I've witnessed it before, with somebody else in another place and time.'

'You mean the Judge, Darren Aubrey?'

'Actually, yes.'

'I've read your book,' Emma smirked. 'He became The Leader, didn't he? He set about that dignity experiment thing to wipe out the elderly because he was molested by an old man or something?'

'You see, in a way I kind of predicted all this with Alex. He is forcing upon others what was forced upon him.'

'Nobody forced him to marry a lesbian,' Emma bluntly pointed out.

'No, you're right, but sometimes we just get carried along by life. Sometimes we're just too weak-willed to alter things.'

'Well he's certainly altered things now, hasn't he!'

'Look Emma,' Peter urged, stepping forward, 'I need your help… Alex needs your help. If he is confronted with you, the one woman who can unearth his heart, we might be able to halt his damage.'

Emma couldn't look at him. She didn't want to face this challenge. 'What a load of bullshit you come out with,' was her wall of a response.

* * *

Peter stepped out onto the street and waited. He knew what was about to happen, The Space had shown him, and he had decided not to fight it. Sure enough a plain white van pulled up beside him and the side door slid open. A puff of smoke was enough to send him to the ground, unconscious. He was scooped up and bundled into the van before it sped off down the road.

Within outward of The Space lay The Cunningham.
Less of pig, but beauty of hind, was good to
Develop and believe that the
Luring of such a being would placate the
Sensual and goad The Two into developing
Through the stage set by Reaping Icon.

And they bore a girl, not a baby.
She was full of mind before her mother
Tore her away and threw her out into the air.
Only then was the dream fulfilled – one of lust and
Loathing, developed to the extent that she could
Deliver wishes beyond mere body.

CULMINATION

I opened my eyes and lifted my head up. There stood Alex – Reaping Icon – looking in at me from beyond my mental tank; my mental concealment. He was holding a blank piece of paper, and presently began to read from it.

'Ostensibly we spent three hours discussing The Space in person very openly.' He looked up at me, raising an eyebrow.

'Ostensibly?' I asked for clarity.

'Something I haven't done with her before. My overwhelming need for her has been reignited.'

'What is this?' I replied, standing up off the floor. Reaping Icon slipped the paper into his jacket pocket, pressing his forehead against the tank.

'Well that's just it, Peter. The opportunity is there for you to utilise such awesome powers. You have consumed your appetiser.'

'The powers of The Space?'

'Powers you have full access to. Tell me, Peter, of this woman.'

'What woman?'

'This woman of which you spoke. The one you spent three hours discussing The Space with.'

'I don't know what you're talking about.' I turned away from him. He merely walked to the other side of my tank so I was facing him again.

'I am in your mind. I know you spoke to this woman, Lauren, about The Space.'

'I did not.'

'To what end? Or, merely for the sake of it maybe?'

'Only once The Space has been over-ruled will an end be revealed,' I blurted out. Reaping Icon was stunned.

'You say rather a lot with so few words,' he whispered.

'I don't know what I'm saying. But I know I've said too much. The Space knows something beyond human thinking. A purpose.'

'The Space is so warm and wondrous,' he pondered aloud, changing his mind. 'You're giving The Space too much personality.'

'How do you know?' I asked.

'I don't.'

'But you're Reaping Icon, you know everything,' I pointed out.

'The Space is the summation of everything that ever was, is or will be. You have access to The Space, so you also know everything.'

'But I'm not Reaping Icon.'

'Are you not?'

'Then assumptions can be presumptuous.'

'I merely suggest the idea that you are wrestling with something that may be an illusion,' he pointed out.

'Do you mean I created The Space?'

He shrugged his shoulders. 'You created me. Except the woman, she didn't. But why speak of The Space with her, Peter? She was not a part of The Great Collective, was she? She is something far beyond that.'

'And what does that reveal about me?'

'I like how you presume the authority to grant me permission to analyse you.' He stepped back from me, his face blank. I stayed silent. 'But It is alive, isn't it? It is more alive than the whole universe put together. That goes beyond personality. You cannot even attempt to comprehend transferring human emotions onto it.'

'Perhaps even we are just not clever enough to comprehend it,' I suggested.

'Don't be silly,' he laughed. 'Calling myself silly... how silly of me.'

'I am not you.'

'You are all of us, Peter. Past, present, future: you are your own parent and your own child. There is you and only ever will be you. You created me, and I am you... you created yourself. Infinite numbers of the same person over and over and over and over.'

'The idea of that is unnerving,' I confided.

'That is why everything is nothing to you. No order, no lies.'

'I plan on usurping that nothingness. Controlling it!' I called out, starting to feel like I was truly Peter Smith again.

'Is that wise?'

'Who knows. I rule the world. Right now, at this very moment in time, I rule the world – the universe. I created the universe! But it's not seen, you don't see it, and that's the crucial thing.'

'How odd,' he responded to my delightful rage. 'Tell me what you told the woman,' he pushed.

'You are Reaping Icon, you already know.'

'To usurp your entirety, Peter, is what I am.'

'I wouldn't want to annoy The Space,' I told him. 'I want to befriend The Space, nurture a relationship.'

'Indeed you do, which is why you told this woman, wasn't it? You told her about The Space because she *is* The Space.'

'We all are – it is everything.'

'And everything is nothing.'

'She is not nothing, she is beyond that. I want an eternity with her.'

He laughed. 'You've no idea what you want. But, revealing your whole self to her scored you nothing.'

'I needed to relinquish myself, give myself over to this life and this life only.'

'Let your humanity flow freely, Peter, let me feel your sickly emotions whizz around in all their crapulence,' he urged, changing gear. I knew exactly what he was trying to do; what he was exceeding at.

'It's true, I feel these things, and I will no longer block them.'

'To no longer block them is to allow me in. Come on Peter, let me usurp your connection to The Space. We will become as one and end humanity's sickness.'

'Very well,' I conceded, ready for Reaping Icon to consume me. But, nothing happened. I stared back at Alex, waiting for him to be relieved of his burden. It did not come. He merely started laughing again.

'Rather too easy,' he said.

'It is what you want... what we want.'

He stepped back from me, clicking his fingers. In came Noose, Ruby and Arthur, who stood either side of Alex and looked across at me. 'What is the worst thing in the world?' he asked me.

'Toilet water splashing up your bum whilst you're having a poo?'

Smiling, he clicked his fingers again and in walked Gary Noose, Katie and Stuart. Noose immediately broke down, collapsing to his knees in an embarrassing sob. 'Oh why, my son, why?'

'Maybe you should ask Peter,' was Gary's reply. 'After all, you were more of a father to him than me.'

'I tried, Gary, I tried.'

'No you didn't. Do you want to know my lasting memory of you?' he spat. 'I must have been about five or six years old. I remember asking you where the birds hide at night. You laughed at me. You just laughed.'

'But,' Noose stuttered, clearing his throat of the choking cries, 'it was so obvious.'

'I was a child, Dad. I was a child and you just laughed at me.'

'But son,' he whimpered, stumbling on his knees to the young murderer, 'they hide from predators at night.'

'But where, Dad, *where*?' Gary squealed like a toe-rag, grabbing his father and throwing him across the room. He slammed into Alex's desk and sent much of what was on it onto the floor.

'In the trees, you dipshit,' Alex growled at him. Gary now went for Alex, who outstretched his hand and placed it on Gary's head. Suddenly all the anger was gone, replaced with terror and shame.

'Please, please,' Gary whimpered, now on his knees, as Alex kept on with the draining. Noose looked over at his dying son, who called to him: 'Dad, help me, I love you.' He couldn't move, he felt like he'd forgotten how to. His mind wasn't on his son, it was on himself. No sign of Gary as an innocent newborn, or an evil rapist and murderer – all Noose could see was himself.

Oddly, Alex suddenly stopped, pulling his hand from Gary's head and taking hold of his hand instead. Pulling Noose's weakened son to his feet, he gave him a hug and whispered in his ear: 'Daddy doesn't love you, but I do.' All at once Gary was a new being altogether, his expression losing all notion of emotion. He looked contented, at one with who he was and what he'd been dealt with in life.

Alex turned to Ruby and Arthur as Katie stepped forward. 'Katie,' he said to her, 'my loving wife.'

'It's Kate now,' was her only response.

'She's a sinner, my loving parents,' Alex yelled at Ruby and Arthur, 'she sleeps with other women.' He turned back to face Kate. 'You dirty bitch,' he went at her, Alex coming out now more than ever. There was still something left of what Reaping Icon had consumed. 'Why bother wasting my time if you wanted women?'

'Fuck off, you twat, I hate you,' she came back at him. He thought back to their first ever kiss, at school all those years ago, and he placed the image in her mind. She'd been so in love, or so she thought, back then. Alex was all she ever wanted... back then. She'd blocked it from her mind, conveniently making it all just go away. But now it had returned, forced upon her. She *had* to deal with it. 'I'm sorry, Alex,' she called out, drowning in her own self-pity. Back then she thought that Alex *was* all she wanted from life. It wasn't to be, he didn't satisfy her. No man could.

'Here is your daughter,' Alex again addressed Ruby and Arthur angrily, 'she is a transgressor of the law. She must be punished.' Ruby and Arthur, so distant from their daughter of late, looked across at her. She seemed unrecognisable to them. The little red-haired girl they'd tried so hard to get and who gave them so much joy had departed this world, replaced by some apparently unreachable miscreant. 'She is not your daughter,' Alex kept on, 'but I *am* your son.' He turned to me and smiled, still addressing them with: 'Do the right thing by me, the one who needs and wants you – denounce this stranger, this criminal.'

I looked over at Ruby and Arthur, who just wanted to die and vanish into the ether instead of facing this. But, this was Reaping Icon, and that *had* to be faced. Their eyes darted back and forth between Kate and Alex, the decision seeming to elude them. They certainly were deeply under Alex's enthral.

'It is a simple choice,' I butted in. They both refused to look at me, but I knew they'd heard me because their sight fell away from Kate and Alex. They stared into space as I finished with: 'In fact, it's not even a choice at all.' I looked over at Kate, as beautiful and as necessary as Ruby. They were my real family

– the family I wanted. But, I had been cast away, never to be accepted back. All I could hope to do now was draw them back together for each other. If only Alex – the original and genuine Alex – could have been a part of that too. Alas, he too, like me, was burdened and bogged down by The Space's curse.

'Surely you don't agree with your daughter's sick, illegal, lifestyle choice?' Alex perked up.

As I watched on, I suddenly became distracted by a tapping at the side of my tank. I ignored it at first, desperate to see my family's problem resolved. But, the gentle yet irritating tapping would not cease. It was almost like a niggling at the back of my mind, that tickling sensation that keeps trying to remind you of things forgotten. I turned to look where the sound was coming from and there stood Stuart. Obviously I had not been keeping an eye on him in the room.

'Hello,' he said quietly, looking a bit forlorn.

'Hi Stuart,' I replied calmly, unable to get at him. I was blocked, my own mentality keeping us physically apart.

'I genuinely am sorry about Lucy,' he said, again with a look of sadness. 'It was a terrible mistake, one I've had to live with at the back of my mind all these years.'

'Only at the back?' I asked him. I'd have thought it'd have been at the forefront constantly. Then again, who was I to talk?

'Is there no way back for us?'

'There's no way back for me.' I turned from him. I would not rise to Reaping Icon's goading. I looked back for Ruby and Arthur, to see them in the midst of an emotional embrace with their daughter. Alex just stared back at me, grinning. And then it came, the full thrashing of Reaping Icon into myself. I was He, and all of He; taking the complete culmination of all those centuries of impending hatred. It felt good... too good. Right now I wanted nothing else but Reaping Icon. Now I was ready to destroy all of eternity. I took hold of The Space, for that was the key to ending things as it *was* everything. We grappled, it not wanting to relent but wishing it had never come to humanity. This itself was a paradox – if I removed The Space from all of this, surely Reaping Icon would never have existed in the first place? No, he came from humanity itself, not the poor naivety of The Space.

Suddenly I caught sight of Noose across the room. There was no tank to contain me now, nothing or nobody but Noose and me. 'Gary murdered Anna's neighbours because of me, Noose, not you,' I called out to him. 'He wanted to bring me out of the woodwork – your surrogate son.'

'But you were already dead at that time, Peter,' Noose called back.

'My inevitable return was already seeding events.'

'So if there had been no possibility of your return... if you were dead full stop... he might not have murdered them?'

I felt The Space go completely from me, from all of mankind, and Reaping Icon and I were the only ones left. The Great Collective, if indeed they'd ever been Great, were certainly no more. There was no possibility of rebirth, no immortal trappings to ever bog me down again.

Alex stumbled next to Noose, yanking a drawer in his desk open and grabbing hold of a gun. He put it to his head and snivelled: 'I don't deserve to live, I'm the one who's sick. What have I done?' But, before he could pull the trigger, Noose snatched the gun from him and pointed it at me.

'You told me to be the one to set you free from The Space's curse,' he said bluntly.

'The Space has gone,' I said.

'Are you free from it?'

'Only in death will I know that,' I answered, closing my eyes and waiting for him to pull the trigger. My desire for him to do that physically easy act was profound. After so long as a yo-yo in life's twisted games, I yearned for my eternal end. The gun fired, and naturally I was numb to its delivery. I waited to drop to the floor, a lifeless corpse. It did not come. I couldn't bear to open my eyes, I wanted them to stay shut forever. They were weeping before they opened, and had I not unsealed them I'd have drowned myself. Noose – Detective Inspector Henry Noose, the best friend I could ever have begged for – was lying dead in a pool of his own blood, a bullet blown clean through his face. His face was gone, he'd removed it with the bullet. I wanted The Space back, it was the only way to drag Noose away from death. It wouldn't come. All I had was Reaping Icon.

I just wanted, *needed*, to wreck terrible misery on everyone now. It had been done to me, so I would do it to them. I caught sight of Stuart again, smiling in his way, and I charged at him. He tried to get away, but it was no good. No human was any match for both Peter Smith and Reaping Icon. Yet, as I punched and kicked him as he cowered on the floor, I wondered why I didn't just remove his life as Reaping Icon. I could utilise myself and take Stuart's being away. That I wasn't doing this gave me a glimmer of a hope that Reaping Icon could actually be cast out and put to an end without me having to die.

I thought of Noose, just lying there, and I rushed over to him. He'd gone from this corpse, no longer to grace me with his kindness. Ruby and Arthur had already left with Kate, and Alex had hold of the gun again. 'I'll do it,' he welched, pointing it loosely at his head.

'Go on then.'

It was missed, and not on purpose,
But on blight of mind and Stages undermined by
Reaping Icon foregone conclusions set in stone,
Crumbled, shifting, forming new Visions.
Scaped that The Cunningham's red herring
Rushed and tore Wiles from the path.

Jolting and joviality could unnerve,
Higher access of inter-outward novelty.

MR MONKEY RETURNS IN:
THE CLONED CLOWN

'To cut a long story short, Superintendent, they're running amok,' Nicola Williams explained. 'And, it's our job to see it's put right before the problem gets out of hand.'

Sergeant Helen Douglas and Officer Jacobs looked on, trying to appear full of pity and sadness at the recent turn of events. They were more in awe than anything else.

'The problem's already out of hand, Williams. We've had three deaths this week alone,' Hastings shouted.

Lauren held up some photos of the three disembowelled victims. 'Deirdre Ann Perrin, mother of Liam Perrin. Queenie Clooney, wife of Colin Clooney and mother to Francesca. Also, a very flattened young paperboy called Samuel Martin, who just happened to get in the way of a speeding reliant robin,' Lauren explained. 'Mrs Perrin was found stabbed and burned. Mrs Clooney was found chopped up into several pieces and placed in various dustbins across town. Poor Master Martin was left where he lay in the hit and run attack. All in all, pretty wicked if you ask me.'

There was a deathly silence before Hastings spoke: 'Colin Clooney. Are you sure?' he asked, deadly serious as he took a gulp.

'Yes, Colin Clooney,' Lauren repeated herself with curiosity, checking the file to make sure she hadn't made a mistake.

'So, he's back,' Hastings gasped.

'Who's back?' Douglas asked.

'The Clown.' Hastings turned away and looked out of the window, sheer horror on his face. 'He's a sick murderer who dresses up as a clown.'

'But,' Jacobs cut in, the top half of his face creased in puzzlement whilst the bottom half sported a big smooth grin, 'I thought he was just legend, just a training college myth?'

'He's not a myth, Jacobs,' Hastings sighed, 'he's more real than you could ever imagine.' He turned back to face the gathering, feeling he owed them at least that much. 'You're too young to remember, but there's somebody who isn't.'

'Who?' asked Douglas, looking over and smiling at Jacobs.

'But, *Sir*,' Williams cut in with some trepidation, 'you can't possibly mean who I think you mean?'

Hastings straightened his back and stared Williams right in the face. 'If The Clown is a playground horror story, then Mr Monkey is a see-saw loaded with TNT,' he growled in defiance.

* * *

'Oh Brendan, you're the man of my dreams! Why are you so amazing?'

'And cut. Excellent, absolutely excellent. Haha, I'll win an oscar for this. Ahem... and the winner for the best director of the year, for his smash hit musical *Mr Monkey: I Am Ace*, is none other than Mr Monkey,' the furry orange sleeve puppet shouted, his flimsy paws swishing from side to side as his body twisted back and to.

Woe is Mr Monkey, for he had sunk to new lows as an unpopular, small town director of an amateur dramatics group who were set to perform an adaptation of Shakespeare's *Romeo and Juliet*. Quite how that had metamorphosed into a musical about the puppet himself was anybody's guess. And, quite frankly, it didn't do to try and guess anything with Mr Monkey around. Second-guessing was even more of a no-no, as it was double a normal guess. Triple-guessing didn't exist. That aside, rehearsals were going well. Comparatively.

'Come on Douglas, stop doddering,' Williams seethed under her breath at her lacking-in-speed sergeant. The dashing Jacobs was already seated and watching the performance with petulant gusto. It annoyed Douglas anyway – he wasn't even a sergeant, yet Williams didn't shout at him. She thought that maybe Williams felt Jacobs didn't have it in him to progress career-wise, and thus wasn't wasting her time pushing him. Nevertheless, she sat down next to him and gave him a smile.

'Sorry,' Douglas mouthed, her mind more on Williams' mental health. Surely she'd been affected by Noose's suicide some weeks prior? After all, everybody knew they'd been on-off lovers for years.

'Sit yourself down,' Williams shouted at the young woman. The small gathering seated on the front row turned around in unison to catch a glimpse of the disturbance behind them. 'Bravo, Bravo,' she roared, applauding the appalling performance they'd just crashed. 'That was amazing, wasn't it Jacobs?'

'Hmm,' Jacobs contemplated.

'So what do you want me back for?' a croaky voice groaned from behind the trio. They turned very slowly to be confronted face-to-face by the iconic legend that was, is and always will be Mr Brendan Monkey. His purple button eyes stared vacantly at them, stitched onto a thinning orange cloth.

'Hello Mr Monkey, how are you?' Williams gulped with trepidation.

'I heard he died,' Mr Monkey said with part sadness and part glee. Williams stared back at the button eyes of the puppet, as cold and as empty as she could.

* * *

'But I killed him myself, I saw his head inflate like a balloon and explode in a gooey guffaw,' Mr Monkey yelled in disbelief, 'then the building collapsed on him and I blew the building up and I put the ashes in a box and blew the box up and-'

'Stop, stop just listen for one minute will you please... just listen,' Williams tried to keep up with him. It was hard trying to stay level with a puppet in a blazing rage at the thought of his worst enemy of all time being back from the dead. He was sure it had been The Clown – the genuine article – who had died that day in the cellar. That was back when everyone believed a copycat clown was at work; could that in fact *now* be the case?

'Okay I'm listening, Nicola. Remember, like last time I was on the force and someone claimed I was too personal with my vendetta against this scum? Oh I was fine at my job; in fact the best and you know it! Douglas and Jacobs told me you still value me as the best. Jacobs even told me that you still believe I'm part of the team, as it were,' he went on, pausing only for an intake of puppet breath. 'Well, I've moved on now. I don't have to kill people to win respect in the neighbourhood. This new town respects me for what I am: a talented artiste... not how many human heads I have on my wall, or however many criminals I come home with. I like it here and I'm not going.' Now would have been an opportune time to fold his arms to elevate his protest, but as he had no control over them they merely continued to hang loosely by his sides.

'Well if you want to hang out with these Shakespearian imbeciles then so be it, but I'm warning you that that personal vendetta thingy might just catch up with you,' Williams shouted back.

'Do you have to shout all the time?' he shouted back.

* * *

'But we can't do it without him. You know he's the best man we've ever and will ever have,' Hastings argued from behind his desk, his fist coming down hard on the top of it. 'And, he's not even a man… he's a puppet, made of cloth. A man of the cloth.'

'I tried to get him to come back but he just wouldn't,' Williams lamented.

'Well you didn't try hard enough,' Hastings growled at her, but she clenched her fists.

'Sometimes I wonder whether you're still fit for your job,' she suddenly came out with, quickly realising she'd said it aloud when Hastings' jaw dropped. She whimpered, gulping, before uttering: 'I'm sorry, Superintendent. I've been under a lot of stress lately.'

'Yes, Henry's death couldn't have helped matters,' he replied acceptingly. 'I believe you two had grown close again just before he did himself in.'

'Well, well, well, isn't this all very lovey dovey? Won't somebody please pass me a bucket,' a voice sounded from the doorway. The pair turned to see Mr Monkey there, his bland unchanging face staring haplessly back at them.

'Mr bloody Monkey,' Hastings sighed happily, 'you old dog, you.'

'I'm a monkey, actually; not a dog.'

Hastings got up and grabbed the puppet's limp paw to shake it. The Superintendent did the old boys secret handshake, winking. 'We need you, Mr Monkey… just like the old days.'

'Then I'm back on the force!' he trilled. Turning to face Williams, he fired: 'Go and put the kettle on, love.'

'Er, what?' Williams tried to clarify, shocked.

Completely ignoring her, Mr Monkey turned back to Hastings and whispered: 'I'll do a deal with ya, big guy,' he giggled, prodding Hastings' stomach with his monkey mouth,

'I get to kill Colin 'The Clown' Clooney and his sidekick Liam 'The Worm' Perrin, and you leave me alone for good,' he suggested.

'A deal,' Hastings replied in haste. 'But you also have to find out what on earth Colin and Liam are up to. You must not attempt to assassinate either of them until you are fully sure of their intentions. We thought The Clown was dead before, but he's somehow risen from the ashes. And as for Liam, well... The Clown hasn't colluded with The Worm for decades. Your job is to stop them progressing and commencing further...' He paused, contemplative. 'They could get close to taking over the world again,' he finished.

'They didn't even come close last time!' Mr Monkey interrupted. 'No, they're too keen on causing awful small-scale pain and suffering, especially The Worm with all his wriggling at the bottom of the garden. I still remember the nursery rhyme that gave a whole generation of children nightmares: there's a worm at the bottom of the garden, and his name is Liam Perrin.'

'Indeed. With the pair of them amalgamating again, we've certainly got our work cut out,' Hastings gasped.

'Then let this be known,' Mr Monkey purred dramatically, 'as the dissolution of that amalgamation!'

* * *

Mr Monkey had arrived in America on the Tuesday last and booked into a paradisiacal hotel in Miami. Although Hastings had told him to stay low, giving the puppet unlimited access to the police treasury had resulted in something quite self-indulgent. Mr Monkey, not being one to take orders seriously, had enjoyed a night on the beach joining in with parties and other forms of entertainment for single men. Later that evening he went back to his rented apartment with Meg, a cocktail bar waitress who had got the innocent puppet and herself drunk.

'An I sad tooo hem fat if he did noot gev me thhe gun I wod kill em all wiff mey water piscal. Bang bang,' Mr Monkey slurred drunkly as Meg dropped her dress to the floor and unclipped her bra. She helped his flimsy body onto the bed as her large exposed breasts glistened in the moonlight.

'Oh Brendan, giv-' Meg stopped as five large men entered the room through different doors and windows. 'Oh my God no,' she screamed, but was silenced when one of the men put a bullet in her head. Her lifeless body slammed to the floor, the fall only slightly cushioned by her loose boobs.

'What haff ya don ya id...id...idiot,' Mr Monkey stammered, trying to get hold of his gun as his vision became weaker and weaker. Four of the men held him down, and the other injected him with a tranquilliser.

* * *

'He awakens to find himself in a mysterious vessel,' a voice announced as Mr Monkey awakened from a dismal sleep. He was in a large, private plane. He tried to move his arms to comfort his aching head, but he found himself strapped to a chair. Unable to move, he peered around the plane through his purple button eyes looking for a body to go with that voice. There was no one in sight, although Mr Monkey's sight was nothing to write home about since that tranquilliser knocked him out some time ago. Plus, his eyes were buttons, not real eyes. What time was it? He looked around, trying to spot a clock.

'It's seven o'clock my friend,' the same voice from before answered Mr Monkey's thoughts.

'How did you know I wanted to know the time?' he asked the mysterious voice.

'I didn't,' it replied. That's funny, Mr Monkey thought. If a person said something that you were thinking, and then you asked them how they knew, the standard reply is: "I can read your mind." Saying: "I didn't" isn't a very substantial answer for the mastermind behind this devilish scheme.

'Good afternoon, Mr Monkey,' a different voice exclaimed, as a metallic door opposite the puppet opened. In the doorframe stood a prematurely grey-haired man. He smiled at Mr Monkey and gently raised an eyebrow.

'Please, call me Brendan,' the puppet replied in his usual confident and defiant voice.

'And you can call me Doctor Bullings,' the man announced.

'And what am I doing here, exactly? Please could you tell me, Dr. Bullfrog,' Mr Monkey giggled.

'Dr. Bullings,' the man yelled.

'Sure it is... Dr. Bullfighter,' Mr Monkey carried on goading.

'Dr. Bullings,' he roared.

'Hey, Dr. Bullface, you're big enough to be a bullfighter yourself. I bet the crowd would go wild when your name was announced at a bull fight," Mr Monkey cheered.

'Arsgghdjjegjrrhgteeeerrrrhgrrrr,' the man screamed as he leapt at the puppet and sent the chair, which Mr Monkey was tied to, flying into the air. He landed, legs first, on the man's shoulders and tried to break his neck with his puppet thighs. Dr. Bullings howled with pain and managed to throw him off and onto the floor. Suddenly the plane dipped down, but almost immediately regained its balance. The plane didn't dip due to Mr Monkey landing with such a thud, however, but because he had managed to pull a wire out of the floor that was sticking up. Dr. Bullings came crashing down onto him and they both cried out.

Meanwhile, on a speeding train below, Ruby and Arthur were having a spot of lunch in a private compartment.

'Oh Arthur, I know things have been tricky of late, but I do feel we've got over the hardest part of our lives now,' Ruby sighed with sweet relief. Arthur rolled his eyes and tucked into a ham sandwich. Ruby filled her mouth with cheese and onion crisps and carried on talking: 'Yup, it's all plain sailing from here on in.'

'Well I suppose all we have left to overcome in life is old age and death,' Arthur replied after some trepidation.

'Help meee,' Dr. Bullings cried out on the plane, as Mr Monkey managed to free one paw and was attempting to garrotte his opponent with the wire out of the floor.

Surprisingly he succeeded, and Dr. Bullings went all limp and died. The puppet now freed himself from the chair. How to get out? When you're thirty thousand feet in the air, there isn't much chance of escape. He picked up a gun from Dr. Bullings' body and bounced over to the door in which the dead medic had made his entrance not so long ago.

He wandered about the plane for some time, his polyester legs dangling with freedom, until he came to a large golden door. There was a large button next to the door, so he pressed it and the door slid open. Behind it was the posh dining area of this obviously luxury plane. A man was sitting on a swivel chair with his back to Mr Monkey.

'We've been expecting you,' the man murmured.

'What do you mean, we? There is only you and myself in here,' Mr Monkey replied.

'Forgive me,' replied the man confidently, 'but I don't get many visitors dropping in for a chat. Let me introduce myself. I am your worst enemy... I am Liam Perrin!' he announced, spinning around in the chair just in time for Mr Monkey to see his mouth close. It was a large mouth, surrounded by an elaborate ginger goatee beard. Gel had helped fashion either tip of the moustache into decorative twirls. Atop the man's narrow head sat an abundance of golden curls, though his hair was shaved at the sides.

The puppet looked startled at first, then pointed the gun at him. 'The Worm! I should have guessed it would be you. Still doing The Clown's dirty work.' He grunted in a monkeyish way, even though he was technically a puppet of an orang-utan. Orang-utans aren't monkeys, but it wasn't wise to try to explain this to Mr Monkey. He wasn't a gibbon either. 'Where is he?'

'Who?' The Worm asked with a big smirk.

'The Clown, you slippery invertebrate,' he demanded angrily.

'I don't know what you mean,' he replied in a calm manner.

'Don't play sweet with me.'

'Would I do that, especially to a man with an unloaded gun?' The Worm quickly pulled out a gun and Mr Monkey tried to shoot him, but no bullets came out. 'What a shame, Brendan. Such a young life to end before his time is up.'

'I'm a puppet, I'm timeless.'

'Timeless, yet fodder for someone else's hand and voice.'

'Liam,' Mr Monkey whispered sweetly, 'if you don't mind me asking, well seeing as you are going to kill me; how exactly have you and Colin The Clown remained hidden for so long until now?' he queried, in a calm sensible manner.

'Well I'd like to think that you went to hell with peace of mind, so I'll tell you.' The Worm smirked as Mr Monkey looked surprised to be getting something out of him so easily. A little too easily. 'The problem arouse when an old lady, very ill lady at that, took me in from an institute I ended up at. She pretended she was my mother and seeing that I had amnesia took advantage of me. I lived with her and Colin lived with his real life wife and daughter. Your section couldn't track us down, and you thought Colin's family was dead so that didn't provide any new lines of inquiry.'

'What a bittersweet tale of woe,' Mr Monkey mocked.

'Yes, well both Colin and I have regained our memories now and we are after you… or should I say were after you.

Colin told me to keep you alive until we landed, but I can't wait that long,' he cackled.

'That Dr. Bullings put up quite a fight just before,' Mr Monkey giggled. 'I soon dispatched him.'

'I just sent him in to soften you up.'

'He must have forgotten the fabric softener,' Mr Monkey chuckled.

'A man of that size is very respected. I picked him up in my old neighbourhood. In fact he's the last piece in the puzzle, or jig-saw shall we say,' The Worm carried on with yet more smirking.

'What do you mean?'

'He was just an innocent man, brainwashed by The Clown and me. We are such master criminals,' he explained with mirth, as he scratched his nose with the barrel of the gun. 'We have been dabbling in science, you see.'

Mr Monkey leapt at The Worm as soon as the gun was pointing away from him. The gun was thrown into the air as they both battled for it. The Worm was fairly wriggly, slipping from the puppet's admittedly flimsy grasp, and he managed to gain the upper hand. He threw Mr Monkey onto the table where his coffee was, this surprisingly allowing him to make a grab for the gun. Sadly, The Worm kicked it out of the way. There was an open door near to Mr Monkey, so he seized the opportunity and jumped through it and into another corridor. The door locked behind him and he rested for a moment, looking around.

There was a pair of double doors marked 'Cargo Hold', which were locked. Looking around for an instrument in which to open the doors with force, a fire extinguisher caught his eye. He picked it up and soon found himself smashing the doors to pieces and entering a very packed room. He looked around for a few moments until he came to his luggage – a briefcase and wrapped parcel. How thoughtful of The Clown and The Worm to bring his belongings along for the ride too.

'Hold it right there Mr,' a husky voice announced behind him. He dropped his briefcase but kept hold of the parcel, slowly turning to face this person. It was a woman, pointing a gun at his furry head.

'Hello Mrs…' Mr Monkey gestured.

'Miss. My name is Kelly Salifield,' she replied with unease. 'Give me your parcel.'

'What a nice offer from a pretty lady,' Mr Monkey laughed. For this, she whacked him across the head with the gun.

'Open it,' she ordered.

'Is that a demand or a come-on?' he asked with absolute honesty.

'Just open it,' she yelled.

He slowly unravelled the neatly wrapped brown box, keeping eye contact with Miss Salifield, and removed the contents of the parcel. It was a red ball.

'What's that?' Miss Salifield demanded.

'A present from home,' Mr Monkey giggled as he threw the small red ball at her. She dropped the gun and caught it with both hands, looking up just in time to see the mischievous puppet protrude one of his purple button eyes and dive behind a large crate of luggage as the red ball exploded, blowing Miss Salifield's hands clean off in the process. She fell to the floor, screaming. Mr Monkey took out yet another red ball and threw it down hard onto the floor of the plane near to the screaming woman. It exploded and made a hole in the plane, causing everything to gush around in a whirlpool. The puppet grabbed hold of his briefcase and hit the cargo door button. The back hatch began to open as the plane dipped down, drastically dropping its height as it neared the ground. The frantic puppet spotted a car near to the hatch. He sat in the driver's seat and placed his briefcase in the passenger's side. There came a groan from the back seat of the car. He turned around to see a stunning young blonde woman lying across the two seats with her arms and feet bound together. Her mouth was gagged. He turned his whole body around to face the girl, removing the gag.

'Get off me, leave me alone,' she cried, struggling to get Mr Monkey away from her. Maybe she was a little puzzled by the puppet's presence. It's not everyday a puppet rescues you, after all.

'I'm on your side,' he argued as he shook the girl softly, 'I'm a prisoner too!'

'I don't take sides,' she shot back, 'and how do I know you're not a part of ARSEN?' the girl shrieked.

'What on earth is ARSEN?' The puzzled puppet queried.

'You mean you don't know?' asked the girl. Mr Monkey thought about raising an eyebrow, but realised he didn't have any. Instead, he protruded one of his purple button eyes again. 'Untie me then.'

'So, I'm on your side. What's ARSEN?' he asked again, as he untied the girl with his mouth.

'This is who we're fighting here – a gang of master criminals.'

'So it's not just The Clown and The Worm then! Who are you?' he wondered. The girl stretched her arms and legs and rubbed the marks on her wrists that the ropes had made.

'Who are *you*?' the girl demanded.

'I'm your only hope of survival… and possibly sexual fulfilment. Now, let's get out of here,' he yelled as the wind from the open hatch had made it difficult for them to hear each other.

'Not through there!' she screamed as he hot-wired the car and got it going. 'Don't tell me we're going through there,' trembled the girl pointing at the open hatch and the vast expanse of sky ahead.

'It's our only chance of escape.'

'*Was* your only chance of escape,' The Worm chuckled as he stood behind the car, holding a gun at the pair.

'You picked up the unloaded gun, wormy boy,' Mr Monkey laughed back at him.

'What?' The Worm murmured as he looked down the barrel of the gun. Mr Monkey thrashed the car into reverse and backed into the slithering cretin, sending him flying through the smashed double doors.

'The gun *is* loaded!' Mr Monkey roared with mirth, satisfied that he had fooled a leading international crook. He changed the gear into forward and proceeded to drive out of the cargo door at the rear of the plane, in mid-air.

'We're thirty thousand feet up, are you mad?' the girl screeched.

'The plane's about to make an emergency landing, I expect we're about a hundred feet at most.' They both found themselves flying out of the back of the plane, screaming as it carried on cutting through the air behind them. The car soon landed on top of a speeding train. 'Just in time to catch the train,' he joked, as he grabbed hold of the girl and leapt out of the convertible onto the top of the train. Suddenly they went under a bridge, the girl seeing it first and pushing Mr Monkey over to avoid him being decapitated. She also ducked just in time, the bridge taking the car with it. 'Stay here and don't move,' he ordered her as he jumped up.

'You're not ordering me about,' she snarled stubbornly. Mr Monkey produced a large coil of rope from his briefcase and tied one end onto a hook on the roof of the train. Suddenly, he felt a pair of hands on his shoulders. Turning around calmly and slowly, he came face to face with a seven foot ape-like creature, in reality a very tough-looking gentleman. This man tossed Mr Monkey off the train like an unwanted toy and ran after the girl. She managed to lose him momentarily, but then tripped as one of her high heels snapped. Mr Monkey held onto the rope as he was hopelessly dragged through a forest of trees and bushes, at a speed of near one hundred miles an hour. The man revealed a knife and began to cut the rope that the poor puppet was so desperately clinging onto. The girl suddenly found herself and picked up the briefcase, slamming the man on the head. He went flying off the train and onto Mr Monkey. Clung he did, pulling the puppet's threads apart with his vast weight as they both struggled with each other. The man lifted his head up just in time to find a large branch off a tree take it clean off. The headless body kept clinging on for about another ten seconds before it caught up with the fact there was no longer a head, then the grip loosened and it dropped away.

The girl hauled Mr Monkey up to safety as he struggled to remain untangled from various twigs and forest shrubbery.

Meanwhile, inside the train below, Ruby and Arthur were still busy eating snacks.

'Sounds like a little disturbance upon the roof, *dearest*,' Arthur exclaimed.

'Oh here we go, what the hell is going to happen to us now?' Ruby growled with indignation.

Above them, Mr Monkey lay on top of the train. The girl could hardly keep her balance as they tore through the air.

'Please be alright, I don't want to be alone again,' cried the girl as she peered at his flat polyester body. He wasn't moving one iota. She turned away to see if anyone was coming. As she did so, the naughty puppet looked up at her. She turned around as he lay still once more. She bent over him and wondered what to do. His mouth was hanging open, so she pushed it together. It fell open again, his fluffy tongue popping out. There was nothing else for it, she gave him the kiss of life. Dear life was instantly restored as he beamed with joy!

'I was gone for a minute,' he feigned, springing up unhurt.

'You, you rotter.' She leapt up from him in disgrace at his toying with her emotions.

'Come on! You're quite the kisser, aren't you?!' he cooed.

'Anyway, we have to get into the train. It's not safe up here on the roof,' he pointed out, grabbing hold of the rope again.

'What do you want me to do?' she asked.

'Stay here, lie down and hold on!' Mr Monkey chuckled.

'Your sense of humour is sickly,' she replied in deadly seriousness.

He bent over the train headfirst, peering into the window. Luckily Ruby and Arthur were too busy fighting over the last bag of crisps to notice the puppet dangling right against their window. Without a word of warning, he somersaulted down the side of the train and leapt underneath it. There was a hatch door in the floor of the train, which he forced open but attempted to keep quiet. As he poked his head into the train he found himself under a table, gazing up a woman's skirt. A sneeze came out of the puppet, instantly sending the woman into a fit of terror. It was Ruby, and suddenly Arthur's boot clacked Mr Monkey in the face and almost sent him tumbling onto the railway track below. The foot came again but this time he grabbed a hold of it. He soon found himself clinging on for dear life once again, this time relying on a foot and a boot. Arthur yelled out in agony as Mr Monkey twisted his ankle to try and get the upper hand. With quite a struggle, he anchored himself up using Arthur's leg and finally found himself safely on the train. He got up from under the table and bounced off. Many passengers were gathered round. They couldn't believe it. Arthur collapsed, clutching his leg.

'You could have broken his leg!' cried Ruby, chasing after Mr Monkey as she looked back at her husband.

'He could have broken my nose... if it was a real nose,' replied the puppet.

'Is that that damn puppet?' Arthur grunted, squinting ahead.

Fighting Ruby back, Mr Monkey opened a hatch in the roof and collected the girl and his briefcase.

'Your fare please, Sir,' asked a ticket conductor behind the puppet. He turned around slowly and found himself face to face with the giant man he'd just fought on the roof. But that couldn't be, surely? He was decapitated by a tree. Mr Monkey gulped as the man brandished a huge sack and grabbed hold of him, tossing him inside and tying a knot in the top.

* * *

Mr Monkey wakened, again on board a plane. It was the same plane as the one before. He was tied to the same chair in the same way. What the hell was going on? Extreme puzzlement was the order of the day. The door in which Dr. Bullings had made his entrance opened. Who walked through it but Nicola Williams. The puppet looked back, astonished. The Worm followed in behind her. Were Mr Monkey's purple button eyes telling him lies? Was this *really* Williams? If so, what was she doing with The Worm?

They stood at each other's side and glared at Mr Monkey with a mixture of mischievousness and stupidity on their faces.

'Well you've completed your training exercise, Brendan,' Williams shouted. Mr Monkey rolled his eyes.

'My training exercise?' questioned the puppet. 'No, no, no, there's something else afoot here… something altogether more sinister than a training exercise.'

'Your mind is void,' she came back at him. 'You were sent on a certain training exercise to see if you could still perform well enough for us. Overall you failed the training.'

'Tell me, Williams, have you joined ARSEN? Have you turned to the evil side of humanity?'

'Oh Mr Monkey,' The Worm laughed, 'so, so foolish. Yes, my foe is once again in my power. How on earth do I do it? I am absolutely wonderful, amazing. I saw the chance to have you in my power yet again and I couldn't resist. So I said why not. But nobody took a blind bit of notice. It's an old saying that, isn't it? You know, a blind bit of notice. The other rebels always ignored me but I rose above them and look at me now. Look where I am!' he roared, but was interrupted by Mr Monkey:

'Yes, you're standing over there.'

'Your time for dying has caught up on you sooner than you imagined, puppet. Other people always think they know best, but they don't because I know best. I am the best. The best in the world. I will own the world. I will own everything in the world, including you,' The Worm yelled, frantically waving his hands about in the air.

'Ah yes, that old chestnut,' Mr Monkey yawned. 'I want to own the world rubbish! We all know that you'll never be Napoleon.'

'Indeed not. Unlike Napoleon, I'll win.'

'Yeah, I'll believe it when I see it.'

'You will not live to witness such an event… as much as I'd like to keep you alive long enough just to gloat. I might keep your purple button eyes as a trophy, mind… I'll have them stitched onto my nightshirt.'

'I doubt I will perish at your hands, not with someone like The Clown standing in your way. You're second to him. He is the leader of your occult group, shall we say. Which ever way you look at it, you will lose in the end.'

The Worm put his hands together and smirked at the bound puppet. 'What if he wasn't with us for much longer?'

'Oh. Oh yes, I see it now. So you kill two people and suddenly every leader in the world abdicates and allows you to dictate their country. Yeah right. Get in the real world dim-wit,' laughed Mr Monkey. 'Are you too scared to let me roam around free, so you have to tie me up? Is that the idea? Oh I thought this was the end of a training session,' Mr Monkey boasted as he waved his head from side to side.

'No, this is just the end,' The Worm announced, as he removed a gun from his pocket and pointed it at his rival. This startled Williams, but she took the initiative and suddenly karate-chopped the gun out of his hand. The whole wall surrounding the three opened up to reveal about fifty scantily-clad young women holding a machine gun each. The Worm looked back at Mr Monkey and smiled, marching out of the circle to leave the two surrounded.

'Untie me you idiot,' the puppet whispered to Williams in a violent tone, turning to protrude an eye at one of the women. She smiled back and cocked her machine gun at him.

'I'm very sorry about all this,' Williams whispered back as she quickly untied him.

'What is going on?' he demanded. 'I am mildly confused!'

'Well, to keep my own life after I was captured, I proceeded in aiding The Worm to get some information out of you. I had to walk in with him and pretend that you had only been on a training exercise,' she explained, holding her head in shame.

'And did he get what he wanted out of me?'

'I doubt it. Probably just thought of a better way. You know, all these women. He has the weird idea you have a weakness for them.'

'I have no weaknesses… except maybe my cotton seams,' he stated firmly.

'Yes, that's why you're tied up here after an unsuccessful escape.'

Williams seemed rather pleased with her jocular statement, though Mr Monkey was not. His paws now free, he stood straight and surveyed the pretty faces around him. 'Maybe I do have a weakness,' he trilled.

'I must be leaving you,' The Worm's voice called out from behind the wall of beauties. 'I eagerly await your entrance at the lair. Everything has been organised for your arrival.' With this, he slipped a parachute onto his back and opened the plane door. 'Tally-ho,' he called back, leaping out.

'There's something fishy about all this,' Mr Monkey remarked, as Williams eyed one of the women up and down. She looked sternly back, pouting her lips.

* * *

'You left them to it on the plane? Can he escape?' inquired The Clown, fuming with circus rage. His bushy red hair fell into tight curls either side of the baldness atop his pale white head. His giant shoes slammed around as he paced up and down.

'Not unless he seduces fifty attractive women,' The Worm replied.

'You fool, he'll be all over them,' The Clown hooted. They were in the headquarters of their hide out. It was dark and murky... until The Worm turned on the lights. The room was huge and spacious, a gigantic conference table filling the majority of it. Despite the massive diameter of the table, only six chairs occupied its circumference. 'How many beans make five?' he pondered momentarily to himself as he counted the chairs.

* * *

'So this is what heaven looks like,' chuckled Mr Monkey. He turned to Williams and whispered: 'Where is the girl that was on the train with me?'

'I don't know.'

'Let's get out of here. What do you say?' He turned to face the girls. 'Hey you,' he called out to one of them, moving closer, 'did you hear what she said about you?' He pointed at another girl. 'She said you had big hips... childbearing hips.' One girl turned to face the other, and Mr Monkey jumped at her machine gun, yanking it from her. 'Now, drop your weapons,' he demanded.

* * *

'It takes us almost ten years to retrieve and rebuild our organisation, get Mr Monkey and have a chance of killing him and what do you do?' The Clown fumed. 'I'll tell you what you do – you leave him with fifty single females on a plane. Why?!!!'

'Don't you dare yell at me!' The Worm half-yelled, half-squirmed back, slipping here and there. 'If it wasn't for me you wouldn't be alive anymore, and those women have had strict orders to assassinate the puppet and his crony.' He waved his fist at The Clown.

'We don't want them dead you stupid idiot, and why does it take fifty to knock him down? Answer me that.'

The Worm whipped a knife out, running at The Clown whilst shouting: 'This is the same knife I killed my poor old mother with.'

'She wasn't your real mum,' The Clown revealed, lifting up his chair and swinging it at The Worm's hand.

'You'll have to do better than that to stop me, you clown,' The Worm proclaimed, ducking out of the way. He threw the knife at his opponent, who caught it in his teeth and spat it out.

'Twenty five years in the circus, wormy boy. I'm unstoppable,' The Clown laughed.

The Worm turned around to grab hold of the chair legs, but The Clown kicked him in the backside. He fell to the floor as The Clown picked up another chair and smashed it over his back. He dropped in a heap as The Clown got out his party whistle and blew it down his ear.

* * *

Mr Monkey stood over the pilot in the cockpit, pressing a gun to his head.

'Tell me where The Worm parachuted to.'

'No,' the pilot replied.

'Where is he?' Williams yelled, grabbing hold of his head and slamming it onto the controls.

'Take it easy, you mad cow,' he whimpered. Williams did it again, the pilot's face now very much ruined. 'Okay, okay. He went to his secret hide-out if you must know.'

'And where's that?' Mr Monkey asked politely.

'I don't know,' he cried, as Williams prepared to smash his face a third time. This time he was telling the truth. 'Please, no. All I know is the co-ordinates where he parachuted out at.'

'That'll have to do, I guess,' Williams sighed, letting go of his head. Mr Monkey turned to her, clearing his throat.

'Gosh, Nicola,' he gulped, 'I wouldn't like to upset you these days. There was a time when you wouldn't have said boo to a goose.'

'Yes, well the geese have flown, Brendan. Experience has taught me to toughen up, otherwise people just piss on you.'

'Here, put this on.' Mr Monkey handed Williams a parachute.

'No. I'm getting too old for this. I'd just hold you back,' Williams replied, pushing it away.

'Nonsense, you're in your prime.'

'No. I'll stay on board, make sure the pilot doesn't try to contact anyone.'

'Okay, you're excused,' he chuckled as he opened the plane door, turning to salute her. 'You're quite a woman, Nicola,' he yelled over the gushing wind. 'You wouldn't hold me back.'

She held her hand out and reached for his paw, a flicker of

193

passion fleetingly floating past. He jumped out, and she pulled the door shut.

'Beautiful tropical islands? How can this be the base for a group of bodging twits?' Mr Monkey asked himself as he peered through his binoculars at the gorgeous unspoilt hideaway ahead. The landing area was a fair sized group of islands joined together by stone bridges. He was still in the air. Suddenly a helicopter appeared out of nowhere, and without a word of warning swooped down, slashing right through the puppet's parachute. It caught up with his tumbling body, getting under him as if to try and mash him up with the blades. It didn't work, for all of a sudden a gust of wind blew the flimsy puppet out of the way and he found himself clutching onto the bottom of the helicopter as it swooped from side to side.

The passenger hatch of the helicopter opened and a foot appeared on the bar right next to Mr Monkey's clutching paws. The passenger was The Worm. He stamped on one of the puppet's paws, forcing him to let go. Now with just one paw clutching on, Mr Monkey found himself severely compromised. The Worm waved his fist in triumph, treading on his other paw. But, this time Mr Monkey kept a firm grip. He wasn't going to give up that easily. Next came a foot to the face for the flailing puppet. He used his other paw to grab hold of The Worm's foot. The pilot of the helicopter pushed The Worm out, and both he and the puppet plummeted towards the depths of the crystal clear water below. But, luckily a piece of his polyester fur got snagged on the rock face as he rushed past, and he found himself dangling from it. Below, The Worm clung onto one of his paws. He flapped the other paw across The Worm's nose, causing him to sneeze.

'Let go,' yelled Mr Monkey, feeling himself literally coming apart at the seams.

'Please don't kill me,' The Worm pleaded.

'Why? After all you've done to me, why should I save your life? Go on, answer that,' Mr Monkey yelled.

'The Clown was the pilot that pushed me out of the helicopter. He wants me dead! I was under his control all this time, I never wanted to be evil. Please, you must believe me,' he sobbed.

Mr Monkey relented, hauling himself and The Worm up onto the top of the rock. He pulled a gun out from under his gaping puppet hole and pointed it at The Worm. 'I don't believe you, but I can't kill a man in cold blood like you can.'

'Can't you?' The Worm laughed, but Mr Monkey protruded a button eye, so he stopped. 'Do you want to know where the helicopter disappeared to?'

'Try me.'

'To my, well our – you know, The Clown and myself – ahem… our secret hideout,' whispered The Worm, covering his mouth with his hands as he looked around to see if anyone could hear him. It was doubtful they could. Even Mr Monkey was having trouble.

'Never!' Mr Monkey feigned shock, his spare paw covering his mouth. 'And where is this hideout thingy of yours?'

'I'll show you.'

'Nice of you to join us. It seems your new friendship has grown to immense proportions,' The Clown's voice announced on the speaker. Mr Monkey shot the speaker, 'Shut up,' casually slipping from between his polyester lips.

They were crawling through a narrow metallic passageway leading to the hideout.

'This is the only other way to get in apart from the helicopter opening,' The Worm pointed out in frustration, struggling to crawl. He was ahead of Mr Monkey, his bum right in the puppet's face.

'Try not to pass wind, please. Anyway, you're The Worm, are you not? Crawling is your forte.'

'Metaphorical crawling... squirming, hiding in the shadows,' he clarified with shame.

'Soon they will be in the capable and tactful hands of myself, The Clown. It's a pity your mother couldn't make it, isn't it Francesca?' sneered the despicable circus act. Francesca, the beauty who Mr Monkey had found tied up on the plane, was tied to one of the chairs around the large table. 'This would have been a nice family reunion if she'd have made it.' He turned to face the girl, honking his red nose and giggling: 'Shame I killed her!'

'Where is this leading to, Wormy? Looks to me like I'm being led on a wild goose chase,' Mr Monkey pointed out as they struggled on.

'We're here,' was The Worm's overjoyed reply, as he came to a halt.

'I don't know why you're so happy. This could be your final resting place,' proclaimed the puppet glibly.

'If it is, then so be it.' He peered through a wire mesh covering the exit from the passageway into the conference room. The Clown turned around and looked right at him, waving and winking. 'Francesca's in there. She's tied up,' he whispered.

'Let's have a look.' He squeezed past The Worm for a closer inspection. 'That's the girl I met on the plane.' Mr Monkey was stunned, giving The Worm the chance to make a grab for the gun as concentration lapsed in the puppet's grip. He snatched it out of his paw, but failed to secure it himself as it fell through a gap in some piping beneath them. Suddenly the whole passage gave way and collapsed, leaving the intrepid pair to tumble to the floor.

'Nice of you to drop in,' The Clown remarked in a disappointedly lacklustre way, perhaps unaware he had missed a rather clever pun.

Mr Monkey stood up and knocked the debris off his fabric body. 'I didn't realise you were such a good comedian as well as an international terrorist,' he sneered.

'There's no end to my talents.'

'There's no beginning either,' Mr Monkey quipped back.

'Takes one to know one's my motto. What's yours?' The Clown queried.

'If you can't beat 'em, join 'em.'

'I think I prefer the motto: if you can't beat 'em, eat 'em,' he roared with laughter. Mr Monkey moved forward. The Clown's tone soon lowered as his finger hovered over a set of buttons on the table. 'Don't be foolish enough to do anything you might regret, Brendan.' He looked over at Francesca, smiling. He became jolly again, giggling. 'I believe you've had a brief encounter with my daughter, Francesca.'

'Just briefly. Our encounter was interrupted,' commented Mr Monkey as he turned to eye The Worm coldly. He smiled at Francesca and she smiled back, but no words were spoken.

'You only got to meet my, shall we say bodyguard, briefly also. Meet Boris, my personal hefty.' The Clown introduced the puppet to a large metallic door, which didn't initially open. Upon clearing his throat, it slid slowly open. At first only smoke came out of the door, but in time a large figure appeared. Who stepped out of the door but the man who had head-butted Mr Monkey on the train. He marched over to Francesca, bending down and kissing her on the forehead, before proceeding to The Clown and saluting him. 'Sit down,' The Clown ordered, pointing to Mr Monkey and The Worm. Boris marched over to them, picking them both up by their necks. He carried them over to the table and plonked them onto a seat each before sitting down between them.

The door in which Boris had entered closed. A smaller door built into it opened. There was no smoke this time, just a frail woman appeared. She had metal hooks instead of hands. With the hooks she carried a tray with six glasses on it. She walked over to the conference table and plonked the glasses down. Mr Monkey took one glance at her and turned away. On further inspection he recognised the woman as Miss Salifield, the woman he thought he'd managed to kill on the plane. She looked a lot older than last time they'd met as well.

'An accident with a pair of balls,' commented The Clown as he glanced at Miss Salifield's hooks.

'And was the significant age increase a bonus too?' Mr Monkey chuckled back. With this, Miss Salifield jumped onto the table and dived for his neck with her sharp silvery hooks. He couldn't move quickly enough to get out of the way, and found Miss Salifield's thighs wrapped around his neck. He tried desperately to swing her off as The Worm jerked forward off his chair to help, but was soon stopped by Boris. She kept on squeezing with pure glee as Francesca cried out for her to stop. Mr Monkey's tongue shot out and he struggled to slip out of her grip, dropping in a heap on the floor next to the collapsed passageway. He picked up a sharp piece of debris and stuck it into Miss Salifields arm. She stopped squeezing as hard. He looked into her eyes and winked, karate-chopping her injured arm. She made a swing for his face with one of her hooks, catching one of his seams and fraying it. He grabbed onto the hook with his mouth and pulled hard at it, managing to pull it off. He now had a dangerous weapon in which to fight with, ramming Miss Salifield out of the way and running past Boris as he jumped onto the table. He was heading to free Francesca, but Boris grabbed hold of his legs and sent him plummeting face first onto the stainless steal-topped table. Poor Mr Monkey gave out a gasp as Boris jumped on top of him and grabbed hold of the hook. The big brute bent the metal hook into a more suitable shape for killing and wrapped it around the puppet's neck.

'Enough,' The Clown commanded. Boris stopped, picking up the choked puppet and tossing him back onto his chair. Before he could attempt to stand again, the seat revealed automatic locking straps similar to those that imprisoned Francesca. The straps locked around Mr Monkey's paws and prevented him from getting up again. 'You've shown yourself to be quite a brutal guy, Mr Monkey.'

'You're not a gentleman yourself, Mr Clooney,' replied the puppet.

'And as for you Liam, you disappoint me,' remarked The Clown, turning to face The Worm. 'Ever the worm, slipping and sliding about... You'll never make a snake, will you?'

'When you throw me out of a helicopter, what do you expect me to do?'

Boris moved from behind Mr Monkey to The Worm, placing his gigantic hands on his shoulders and pressing down. The Worm was crushed in his seat, squirming and wriggling about as he begged for mercy.

'I pushed you out of that helicopter for one very amiable reason – you delivered Mr Monkey to me without me even risking a hair on my head.' The Clown ran his fingers through his tight bright red curls. 'Ingenious, isn't it?!' He sneered at a job well done.

'Quite,' the puppet replied, 'but why do you need me?'

'Ah yes, let me think...' The Clown answered calmly, 'maybe because you're trying to kill me!' he yelled, pulling an impossibly tiny bicycle from his jacket pocket and riding it around the room. 'Now listen here you stupid little puppet, I've had the chance to kill you thousands of times in the past. But no idiotic, buffoonish loonaticic imbasillic nickumpoopish mastermind of the century Colin "The Clown" Clooney spares your life just because he's got a soft spot for you,' he finished, jumping off the bicycle and leaping through the wall, which happened to be made of paper in that specific spot. He poked his head back through the hole he'd made, pointing his finger frantically at Mr Monkey.

'Number one, it's rude to point. Number two, please learn to count. At most you've had three chances to kill me,' the puppet cleared.

'Seven, actually,' The Clown confirmed, calming down as his huge floppy feet stepped through the hole. He was excited at the thought of having somebody with as much improvisation and wit in them to crack a mastermind such as he. If anything, he adored the puppet. He saw him as his only worthy adversary. 'We've had our moments together,' he said with warmth.

'I do believe we've shared some moments, too,' The Worm butted in.

'Ah yes, we have,' The Clown sighed, his life wasted with The Worm. He didn't even glance at him. He was too busy watching Mr Monkey get interrupted by Francesca's beauty. 'You enjoy women, don't you Brendan?' He stepped up to his daughter with a seedy grin.

'Well I can't help noticing that she is very attractive… especially for something that came from your genitalia.'

'Perhaps you want to see more of her? I wouldn't want your final hours to be so, shall we say, restless. I'd like to know you were doing something constructive,' The Clown tittered. He was in his absolute element, he couldn't even be happier putting a spider in his sister's purse.

'You're sick in the head, you're no dad to me,' Francesca cried out.

'Everything's gone to pot. I can't believe it. Get me out of here. I'm supposed to be your partner. Are you too scared to release me? Scared of what I'll do. Haha,' The Worm suddenly ranted as he twisted and turned in his chair.

'Oh shut up,' everybody shouted at him in unison.

'Tell me, if I am to die, what does ARSEN mean?' Mr Monkey just came straight out with it. He thought it best not to play with The Clown's mind too much at this stage in the jigsaw.

'Ah yes. Baby always comes back to its mother, doesn't it? A bird back to it's old nest. A frog back to the pond in which it was once a tadpole. Now let me see, ARSEN. Where have I seen that before? Arsenal? No. Oh yes, I know now. ARSEN stands for; All Rudiments Should Evolve Nicely!' The Clown proclaimed. There was a pause as Mr Monkey puzzled over it.

Finally, with some hesitation, he asked: 'What does that mean?'

'You like asking questions, don't you?' The Clown had no reply off the puppet, so he continued. 'Well, let me take you on a journey. Not in space. Not under the sea, well it is under the ground. Even further under than we are now. Let me show you.' He nodded to Boris to press a switch on the wall by where Miss Salifield lay unconscious. Without a word of warning, just a grin from Boris, the entire floor proceeded to move downwards. The Worm remarked that the idea of the floor moving down was his and not The Clown's.   They fell into darkness… down, down, down. The lowering floor stopped, and both Mr Monkey and Francesca were curious to see where they had ended up.

'Now, Mr Monkey,' The Clown announced proudly.

'Yes, Mr Clooney?'

'Ahem. Now, I introduce to you level ARSEN of my empire. This is purely for your benefit, Mr Monkey, in seeing how your body, after your use of it, will go to helping my kingdom – my kingdom of workaholics where I am their leader… where I give them instructions on what to do in life, or shall we say what to do in Zombie.' He paused, waiting for a small chuckle from his guests due to his brilliant wise crack made prior. There was nothing. He sighed and his shoulders fell. The wall facing Mr

Monkey began to disappear into the floor and The Clown introduced a devilish looking device to the group. 'Behold, the ultimate cloning machine.' The device in question looked quite sinister. There was a large table-like surface area in which a perspex cubical stood on top. Towering above all that was an indescribable pole-shaped metal item. About two metres away was exactly the same again. Like a mirror image, except the opposite way round, so the poles were as close together as possible. All in all it resembled some kind of grotesque Victorian experiment.

'Cloning device?' Mr Monkey sighed. 'Laaaaame.'

'Yes well, watch this.' He clicked his fingers at Boris, who picked Miss Salifield up and carried her over to the device. The left cubicle rose, and he tossed her in. It lowered on top of her and The Clown outstretched his hand, showing the group a ring on his wedding finger. He pressed a small red button on the top of the ring and suddenly a slurping noise sounded. A pile of peach-coloured goo splattered from the top to the bottom of the right cubicle, before a flash of light blinded the onlookers. When it had faded, to their astonishment, there stood a second Miss Salifield in the right cubicle. She even had hands again. The original version, sans hands, still lay slumped in the left one. 'Ingenious, isn't it?'

'That's impossible,' Mr Monkey responded in awe, 'it must be one of your circus tricks.'

'You were the one that wanted to know about ARSEN. The Worm can back me up.'

'I'll kick you in the back once I'm out of this chair,' was The Worm's angry response.

'What do you need me for, Clown?' The puppet was beginning to get uneasy now.

'You're the one I've chosen for cloning. Your physical and mental strength will bring credit to my evil team,' he stated with menace.

'Oh, no. No, no. You're not cloning me. No, no,' Mr Monkey stuttered, shaking his head. Without even a hint to him, Boris clacked his head with his fist, sending the poor thing into an unconscious daze.

* * *

Mr Monkey awakened upright in the so-called "cloning dome". He struggled to move but was unable to do so. The Clown appeared in front of the cubicle.

'Ingenious, isn't it?' The pesky pale-faced one looked pleased with himself.

'What on earth do you want to clone me for?' Mr Monkey queried, curious.

'I've already told you.'

'Very evasive, aren't you?' Mr Monkey snapped.

'You do lack courage in your conviction, Mr Monkey. Sit back, well, stand back, and let nature take its course,' The Clown upbraided softly.

'So I'm being used as a scapegoat for the horrible memories you have of your brutal childhood in which the evil of your mind was founded?' Mr Monkey snapped back firmly.

The Clown spoke no more. He stared blankly at the puppet for a time, before suddenly disappearing from view. Mr Monkey attempted to move his head to see where he'd disappeared to. He couldn't. The conference room was no longer in sight. The cavity wall which concealed the cloning laboratory must have been replaced.

Mr Monkey had seldom been in such a precarious position that didn't end up with him coming out on top. In fact, as he reminisced about the past, he had always come out on top. His wits had always got him out of trouble at the end of the day.

The Clown re-appeared, tittering to himself as he pointed a remote controlled device at his opponent.

'What do you hope to achieve by this?'

'Now let me consult my evil scheme book,' The Clown giggled. 'Ah yes. I plan world domination, with you as my puppet.' He had not consulted his diary at all. He merely scratched his head.

'Why, Clown, why?!' Mr Monkey despaired.

'So many questions, so little time. Boo hoo, sob sob,' The Clown lamented. 'I will merely use your clone for random tasks that will involve your face to make an appearance. As for your body and its contents, well... You're just hollow inside,' he sighed.

'Ya what?' Mr Monkey yelled.

'I think you'll find the term is, "what did you say?" not, "ya what?" or whatever inscription you polluted the English language with.'

'Oh why don't you just go ahead and clone me you beastly failure of the anatomy,' blabbed Mr Monkey.

'Nice to see a happy clone, just like Nicola,' smirked The Clown.

'Nicola? You mean...'

'Indeed! The Nicola you met on the plane was a clone that I created. Pretty good, don't you think?' The Clown raved.

Mr Monkey didn't believe for one moment that The Clown spoke the truth, but he continued to play along with him nonetheless: 'So all that rubbish with Nicola was to lead me to you!!!'

'Bravo Sherlock, bravo,' The Clown sang whilst clapping his hands in melody.

'The Worm in on it too?'

'Not quite, but I won't tell all at these early stages of what will build up to be a huge and long-lasting friendship...'

'Not if I can 'elp it.'

'Well, can't stick around gossiping all day you know. People to kill, places to blow up. A busy schedule, you do understand,'

The Clown flabbed, tightening his face up and nodding.

'I fully understand.'

The Clown spoke no more, just pressing a button on the remote he held in his hand. As previously, the two poles connected with electricity. Mr Monkey felt a power surge run down his body and ignite at the base – his whole being becoming the subject of frequent uncontrollable spasms. Something started to go wrong. The straps inside the dome holding his paws burst open and, although in terrible pain, he managed to free himself from the remaining straps.

The Clown began to shake and dropped the remote, prompting Mr Monkey to bang his shoulder against the cubicle. Nothing happened. He roared in anger and thrashed at it, shattering it into a million pieces. The Clown stood paralysed with amazement as the puppet came tumbling down with the glass and thrust his body onto The Clown. The two of them went flying through the metal wall, Mr Monkey using his arch-nemesis as a shield. The two men found themselves tumbling down about fifty feet until the both of them landed on top of each other on a large conveyor belt which was moving towards a large pit where quarry rock was falling down. Glass and metal came crashing down on top of them. They lay unconscious as they moved closer towards the pit, the huge rocks falling another twenty feet into giant gnawing metal mincers and being torn to pebbles.

Mr Monkey lay unconscious, but The Clown was awake. The drab circus menace had sustained minor back injuries but was able to haul himself away from the orange one, and further up the conveyor belt. It kept on sliding along, carrying the pair to their impending demise. And what a demise! The Clown grabbed onto the side of the conveyor belt, desperate to get off and save his pale skin. Suddenly Mr Monkey grabbed hold of his foot, trying to pull him back. However, he found his less than energised body clinging onto The Clown's foot for dear life as he now dangled over the edge of the pit.

'Give it up, puppet. You've lost,' cried The Clown in anger.

'I never lose, *Colin*,' he called back with newfound strength in his voice.

'Doesn't look like you're in much of a position to contradict me, *Brendan*,' he called back hastily. Without any further hold up, Mr Monkey proceeded to pull himself up using The Clown. 'You stupid fool, my arm's dislocated,' he screamed out in pain as the puppet hoisted himself up onto his back. The Clown was horrified by the prospect of his body being used as a weapon against him, and Mr Monkey soon found himself balancing on the edge of the belt, clinging onto the safety bars either side. His enemy was still holding onto his own hook of a handle. This was the last ever hope of either of them staying alive, as, after building up enough energy, Mr Monkey grabbed hold of The Clown's fingers with his mouth. He no longer showed his pain – just a tightening of the jaw.

'Time for some truth,' Mr Monkey growled.

'Remarkable, isn't it?' The Clown replied, sounding remorseful of something.

'What is?'

'That I can manipulate you into being the weak, understanding type – the type that keeps his worse enemy alive to ask him some petty questions. Well you should have killed me when you had the chance,' he sneered as he looked behind the puppet.

'What do you mean?' he demanded, turning around, thinking that The Clown was probably just trying to talk his way out of this situation. But, he came face to face with Boris. The shock and sheer surprise of seeing him gave him a start, but it was the blow to the head from Boris that sent him head-first into the pit. Luckily, some of his polyester fur snagged on a jagged edge and he found himself staring down into the pit as huge rocks were mashed into dust by the gigantic metal teeth. Boris lifted up a rock off the conveyor belt and launched it at Mr Monkey. It hit him on the head, but he managed to clamp his paw onto a hook as a second rock hit him. Boris pulled his boss up and helped him to safety, as the poor puppet continued to dangle helplessly. Boris smiled and then stretched his arms to indicate a heavy weight needing to be lifted. With not a word being spoken, Boris bent down over the pit and lifted Mr Monkey's paw off the hook. His whole life now depended on Boris letting his paw go as he dangled to and fro. It was up to Mr Monkey to amend the evil. With his free paw, he took the initiative and swung it, smacking Boris hard in the face. He seemed surprised, but not hurt in the slightest. As he let go of the paw, the other hooked around his neck and Boris lost his balance. He came down with a bang onto the conveyor belt and Mr Monkey swung himself around, grabbing a hold of the same hook that The Clown had previously grown accustomed to. Boris found himself in the same position as the puppet had once been in – dangling from a hook by his foot.

'Alas, it's time to bid adieu!' Mr Monkey quipped, slapping Boris in the face with his free paw and causing him to lose his grip. He went plummeting into the razor sharp blades beneath him. Mr Monkey couldn't bear to watch what evil self-defence he had just performed – the splatter of blood on his face being the only hard evidence that justice had been served.

Rocks still came crashing down, but our hero pulled himself up into a safer position and looked around for that children's entertainment menace. He was nowhere to be seen. The room was large, but almost empty. A huge hole at the other end of the conveyor belt where the rocks poured in seemed the main feature. One side of the conveyor belt was almost up against a wall, and the hole in which Mr Monkey had made his entrance could be seen.

He got himself off the conveyor belt, casually wiping off some of Boris's blood. He spotted a set of double sliding doors. It must have been an elevator of some sort – it must have been The Clown's escape route. Gaining entry into it was a challenge in itself, especially for a half-disorientated heap... smeared in blood and gore.

The fact that the challenge of getting into the elevator was met with considerable ease escaped his mind. A single button, marked "PRESS ME", sat on the wall. He pressed it, entering. In the elevator was one small button. He pressed this too. It began to move. Which way? Up, down... sideways... it could not be told. And then, it abruptly stopped. The automatic doors sprang open. Mr Monkey saw before him a huge circus centre ring. He skimmed the room curiously and then spoke: 'Clown, my faithful foe. Having a little game are we?' Not expecting a reply, he turned to face the elevator door. It had closed and there was no way out of the circus now.

After a cacophony of clatter, and some whistles, The Clown rode into the centre of the circle on his unicycle – juggling balls of fire.

'Years I've waited, puppet – years. Sets of 365 days!!! I wanted you, the man who thwarted my plans last time, to be the first one to see them back in action. Only this time, I won't fail!' The Clown laughed hysterically, his pedalling intensifying as the glow of the flaming balls brightened. 'And you will be dead... DEAD! No more will you solve the crimes I commit.'

'I've solved my fair share of crimes in my time.'

'You've committed your fair share of crimes too,' The Clown pointed out. He was right too. 'I became a clown to entertain children, old foe... but you, *you* became a crime solver to ease your guilt at committing so much of it. You're as bad as me. No, you're worse. I can admit what I am.'

Mr Monkey turned and looked in the reflective surface of

the metallic elevator doors and saw his own reflection – my reflection. I saw Peter Smith. Peter Smith was an orange sleeve puppet.

'Join me, puppet,' The Clown's voice called out. I turned back to face him; it was Reaping Icon. 'Humanity should pay for the sickness it has caused. Let's stamp it out. Join ARSEN and let's burn the universe.'

'We are already one, there is no need for me to join.'

'I am not calling you, I am calling *as* you. The far future is what I beckon forth with my brightly varnished lips – our lips. Oh the hilarity!' The Clown cackled, suddenly hiccuping. He leapt off his unicycle and threw the fire balls into the air, catching each one in his mouth and swallowing them as they came back down. He burped, breathing fire all over the puppet's polyester fur. Sadly it was not fire retardant, and he instantly burst into flames. 'Doom... DOOM! Hellish, hellish doom, you ridiculous thing!' The Clown screamed as Mr Monkey rolled about the floor in agony. He jumped about in his huge polished yellow shoes, honking his big red nose. Suddenly his chest burst open, splattering blood all over the puppet and dampening the flames. Francesca came into view, clutching a machine gun as she filled her father with bullets from behind. He stumbled forward, arms outstretched, before managing to turn to face his executioner. When he saw that it was his own daughter, he smiled and cried: 'You've done me proud, child,' before she put one final set of bullets in his head and sent him slamming to the floor on top of Mr Monkey.

She dropped the gun, horrified with herself, and ran over to pull the puppet from beneath her dead dad. His bullet-riddled, clown-costumed corpse resisted release of the man of cloth at first, but with a good hard tug Francesca managed to pull him out. It was no good, however... he was just too badly burnt. His once vibrant purple button eyes were melted beyond recognition, and the rest of his face was just a charred rag now. She dropped to her knees, sobbing. Mr Monkey was gone.

The next day I went to the shop and bought another orange sleeve puppet monkey, and slipped my hand into it.

Laughter and the faint murmur of a cackle,
Came and came and went again.

COMPLETION

(FORTY YEARS LATER)

'Goodness sake, Mother, why can't I watch what I want to for a change?' Peter babbled to himself as his grey, wrinkled face flanged about. He lay on his deathbed, his senile mind all over the place. Visions of long ago occupied his decaying mind – but not *that* long ago... only in this lifetime. He'd had a full life this time, however, and had soared past thirty-six. He had broken free from the trap, escaped the endlessness of incessant rebirth. He would have felt himself lucky, had the dementia of old age not altered his perceptions beyond repair.

'Oh it's just awful seeing him like this,' Lauren cried, holding his hand. Chloe patted her mother on the back.

'Don't worry about it, Mum, this is life.'

'Noose!' Peter called out, gasping for breath. He pulled his hand from his wife's and outstretched it towards the bedroom door. After taking one final intake of breath, the old man gasped: 'I can see you. You came for me, Noose,' before exhaling the last of the air from his lungs and dying. His hand fell to the bed, where Lauren clutched it once more.

'Oh I love you, Peter, forever I love you.'